GIDEON RISING

BOOK 1

MANIPULATION

Written by SALACIOUS

SALACIOUSBOOKS.COM

Copyright © 2021 By Salacious @salaciousbooks.com

Gideon Rising Manipulation and The **Gideon Rising** series are a work of fiction. Names, characters, situations and circumstances are the products of the author's imagination. Any resemblance to actual events, persons, or locales, is entirely by coincidence.

Author - Salacious
Cover illustration - Jayna Simpson@paintedplanet.org
Editor - Pamela Landsberg

To Join our mailing list for future updates, visit:
Salaciousbooks.com

Author's revised first edition
ISBN# 978-1-7366644-0-7 (ebook), 978-1-7366644-1-4 (paperback)

10 9 8 7 6 5 4 3 2 1

Table of Contents

PROLOGUE

The moonbeam seeping in from the window casts just enough light for him to finish his work. There's no more bleeding; she's gone. She shed her body as fast as she shed her clothes. Eager for him to take her, just not in this manner.

Picturesque against the blood-stained sheets, shades of red perfectly frame her nude, lifeless body.

By inserting angiocaths in the veins all around her, it enabled him to equalize the flow of blood, creating a lovely aura effect. Her milky skin adds an unexpected bang, almost worth the price of dinner.

Something's missing...the red lipstick. He retrieves it from her purse.

Kneeling beside her, he carefully drags it across her full lips. The true red complements her glassy blue eyes.

Fiddling with the concealed button on his sleeve, he presses down, twisting counter-clockwise. The button pops away from its base, exposing the razor-sharp metal stamp hidden below.

Turning her head slightly, he holds the stamp against the front of her ear canal, and presses it deep into the flesh. The image is undetectable. *It's perfect.*

As dawn approaches, he takes photographs, then gathers all shreds of the evening into a trash bag.

Opening the door, he pauses to look back one last time. *She's lucky it was me. She'll be remembered for a sensational end.*

He makes his way back to the city. Back to his phony life.

DETECTIVE CHASE

As Stan pulls into the parking lot, he sees it. Yellow tape. Made from the thinnest plastic, it's incredibly effective at holding back hordes of people.

Shoving through the group of reporters, he flashes his badge at the officer standing guard. The officer waves him through. Stan ducks under the barrier, then sees Mack, the department photographer. Making his way back to the parking lot the two men cross paths. Mack mumbles under his breath, "Prepare yourself. This one's a doozey."

Stan heads up the stairs to the third floor. By the time he reaches it he's winded. He notices there are no security cameras around the building. *Probably why he picked this dive...*

He flashes his badge at the officer posted outside door 305.

"Detective Chase."

The officer opens the makeshift barricade, allowing him to pass.

The room feels hot. A young officer stands in the shadows in the corner of the room. The look on his face tells Stan this is his first time. He'd like to say it gets easier, but he'd be lying.

Stan looks at the blue sheet draped over the bed. No need to ask what's underneath it.

Surprised to see Fish on scene, he says, "Fancy seeing you here. I don't think I've ever seen you out of the freezer."

"Capt'n said this one's a bit messy, asked if I'd come down and take over."

Stan tilts his head toward the covered lump. "How long?"

"By the looks of rigor, not more than six to eight hours. I'll know more when we take her in. As of now, she's a Jane Doe."

Fish instructs his team to cover the floor with plastic sheeting.

"Lay it under the bed and the surrounding floor."

Stan watches the forensic team carefully lift the bed just enough to slip the plastic sheets underneath it without disturbing the corpse.

"Move the bed away from the wall. We don't want to stain the paint."

It occurs to Stan they use plastic to keep from tracking blood, but he doesn't see any.

Fish turns his attention to Stan. "You sure you want to see this? It's pretty grim."

Stan nods hesitantly.

Fish peels back the blue sheet. The woman is lying in a pool of blood.

"Dear God," whispers Stan. He takes two steps back and looks down at his shoes. It's no secret, his hating the sight of blood. A fact that every cop in his department teases him about, given his chosen profession.

The team works in unison as they carefully pull the fitted sheet from the mattress.

"All right, all together...slowly now."

Holding onto the sheet, they proceed to lift the body. A thick syrup of crimson drips onto the blood-soaked mattress. The smell is sickening.

In the twenty years he's been with the unit, Stan's never seen such a thing. His eyes track the trails of blood as they suspend the woman's body.

Fish reaches under the midsection to help move the corpse to the floor.

Having set it down, Fish tears off his blood-soaked paper robe. "Thank goodness for spill proof."

Stan moves in to get a closer look before they bag her up. Her skin is unusually white, making her red lipstick stand out. *Red lipstick...*

As he scans the body, he notices, along with being tapped out, she's got burn marks on her wrists.

"She looks to have been tied up for a while."

"Not to mention a punching bag for an angry dick," says Fish, pointing to the bruises on her thighs.

Stan points to the lipstick, "Unsmudged, still vivid, hardly what you'd expect to see on a dead woman. What do you make of it?"

Fish looks closer. "It looks to have been applied post mortem. We can have it analyzed, but it'd be a needle in a haystack trying to source it."

Finding the brand of lipstick isn't nearly as important to Stan as learning it was placed after the woman's death. *What does it say about her killer?*

A man's voice heckles near the door, "There aren't going to be any more single women left in this town with this nut-job on the loose."

Fish and Stan turn toward two rookie officers ogling the crime scene.

"Show some god damn respect and get the hell out!" snaps Stan.

Startled, the officers back out of sight. Stan shakes his head. "What the hell is wrong with people?" He pulls a bottle of anti-nausea pills from his coat pocket, then pops one in his mouth.

"I'll check with the night manager and go through the guest list. Someone may have seen or heard something that can help us."

As the team finishes bagging the body, Fish utters to Stan, "This kind of thing always perplexes me. What makes a man do something like this?"

THE ACCIDENT
(12 years earlier)

Glancing over her shoulder from the front seat, Bella asks, "You okay, honey?"

Her son's eyes dart to his mother's shiny red lips, then to her raven black hair. She reminds him of Snow White.

"I'm hungry."

His mother reaches for the bag of snacks she'd packed for the drive, muttering, "I don't care for this road, Vic. So many blind spots."

Her husband says reassuringly, "The turnoff should be coming up any time now."

The car climbs steeply up the hill, then drops sharply. Gideon feels butterflies rise and fall in his belly. "Whoop-dee-do!" he squeals.

Mr. Damascus chuckles. He smiles at his son in the rear view mirror, wondering, *where did Gideon learn that word?*

Bella releases her seat belt to reach back and hand Gideon his animal crackers, "Let's just hope we get to the lake before--"

--everything goes black. There's a deafening silence, shadowed by a suspended sensation, and then the volume comes back on. A far off howling in the back of Gideon's mind becomes louder and louder. As it moves to the forefront of his consciousness, it evolves into a persistent screaming in the dark that hurts his ears.

He opens his eyes to find the car filling with smoke. His left eye stings. The world is blurry. The air is thick; it makes him cough.

Disoriented, his body slumps heavily against the left side of his car seat. A man appears, wearing a yellow jacket and a big metal hat. His face is red and scrunched. It frightens Gideon. He screams.

The Fire Captain's voice is calm as he unclips the straps on the child's car seat.

"It's all right, son. Let's just get you out of here."

Big hands lift Gideon out of his seat. The man holds him up and another man grabs his arms. As he's pulled out of the vehicle, Gideon sees his daddy's car is on its side. Another car is bashed into it. Both are on fire. He looks for his parents and catches sight of his mother's shoe lying in the dirt. Confused, he kicks hard, trying to break free.

"Easy, little fella."

The fireman holding him asks, "You want me to call the paramedic over to look at his eye, Cap?"

Climbing out of the vehicle, the Captain says, "No, they've got their hands full. I'll take him over to the Sergeant."

He reaches out to the small boy.

As Gideon slides back into the Captain's arms, he sees two men in white kneeling beside his mother. Her pretty face is masked in blood. The top of her white dress is covered in red smudges.

"Momma!"

As the Captain turns away from the vehicles, Gideon quickly glances over his shoulder, attempting to see what's happening to his mother.

A loud explosion startles him, making his body jolt and his head hurt. He screams. The captain quickly scuttles in the opposite direction.

Sobbing, Gideon cranes his neck, straining to see around the brim of the Captain's hat. Carrying his mother on a stretcher, the men in white scurry away from the burning vehicles. They set her down alongside the road. One of the men drapes a blanket over her, covering her face.

"Momma! Momma!" Gideon sobs as he calls out to her again and again.

The captain comes to a halt and yells, "Tell them to hurry it up with the line and get those reporters out of here!" He looks to Josh, a junior fireman standing thirty feet away and yells, "Tell those reporters to move back. Remind them not to photograph the minor. We can't have him plastered all over the news."

Josh rushes off to carry out his instructions.

Another firefighter approaches. "Engine five is two minutes out. Gee, that's a nasty cut for a little guy."

The Captain gives him a stern look. "The paramedics will take care of it. Don't call his attention to it."

"Oh, yeah, right. It's probably not as bad as it looks. You know how eyes are, one little scratch--"

The Captain glares at him, cutting the dimwit off. "Help Josh and those two officers push the line of reporters back."

A dozen firemen rush past them, carrying heavy fire hose. Gideon looks back over his shoulder and sees there are now several stretchers beside the road. All are covered with blankets.

He screams for his mother, straining to get down, but the fireman moves farther and farther away.

Kicking frantically, he punches the man in the face. The Captain shifts Gideon's body upward, forcing him higher up on his shoulder. Gideon cries, "Down, I want down!" His voice is drowned out by a second fire truck screaming toward them.

Frustrated, he screams for his father, "Daddy! Daa-dee!"

Up ahead he catches a glimpse of his dad yelling at two police officers. Gideon calls out as loud as he can. His father turns toward him; the angry look on his face changes to one of relief, and he holds his arms out to him.

"Gideon, oh, thank God."

The Captain hands the boy to his father.

Victor cradles his son to his chest, rocking him gently.

"You'd better have that cut looked at. He's probably going to need stitches."

Victor's anguished face looks up at the Captain and nods. His voice breaks as he struggles to say a heartfelt, "Thank you."

The Captain's big hand gently strokes Gideon's wet cheek as he says, "We can be grateful for small miracles, especially when they show up in the worst situations." He turns to walk away, then stops and turns toward Victor.

Reaching into his pocket, he says, "I'm very sorry for your loss, Mr. Damascus. If there's anything we can do, any reports you need, just call the station."

He hands him his card with the station number.

Victor watches him head off in the direction of the burning vehicles.

Gideon sobs pitifully into his father's neck. "Daddy, mommy's not waking up. I want my mommy--"

--the pain in Gideon's chest is unbearable. His eyes sting. Shutting them tight, he holds his breath. The siren seems louder somehow, screaming all around, making his head ache intensely. The grogginess begins to fade and gradually he remembers where he is. He gets up and rushes over to the alarm clock to shut it off.

Rubbing his palms over his eyes he wonders, *God, it's been twelve years...will I ever stop dreaming about the accident?*

Trudging to his closet, he meanders around the tall stacks of old textbooks.

Opening his closet door, he pushes his shirts aside, then flips up the blank electrical panel at the back wall. Reaching into the hole, he lifts his journal and pulls it out carefully so as not to upset his vials or the glass syringes next to it.

Meandering to his desk, he sits down and lightly taps his pen to his temple. It only takes a moment of reflection before jotting down his thoughts:

It's possible when passing on gossip to a stranger, (something useful), gaining the person's trust is easy. After that, they'll believe just about anything.

Setting down his pen, he returns to his closet to carefully place the journal back inside its hiding place. Tugging a shirt off a hanger, he gets dressed for school.

Gideon picks up his backpack then opens his bedroom door. He hears rap music playing downstairs. It isn't unlike Shelly to leave the music on, but she never listens to rap. *She's probably passed out in the living room again.* She kept him awake partying all night with her druggie friends.

Gideon wonders if her guests ate any of the chocolates? His step-mother's diligent calorie counting only allots for booze, yet her boyfriends shove three or four chocolates in their mouths at once.

If they knew the candies were laced with salmonella, would they still eat them? Gideon thinks back to last week's fucknuts. *Odie and Tank, sure, they're both that stupid. And then there's Olivia...Shelly's drug dealer.* Gideon ponders how much money Shelly spends on diet pills and crack.

Descending the the stairs, he sees clothing on the floor in a trail from the entryway. One of the garments is an unmistakable pair of men's jeans. *Aw hell! One of the dick-wads is still here.*

He turns left and pushes past the swinging doors into the kitchen. He hasn't eaten since yesterday morning. Opening the fridge, he finds a bottle of vodka and a loaf of bread. Nothing else. He uncaps the bottle, then dumps the contents down the sink.

He checks the date on the bread. Only two days past its expiration. Shoving two slices in his mouth, he twists the bag and replaces the plastic pick.

On his way to the front door, Gideon tosses his backpack over his shoulders, then something catches his eye.

He turns his head to see a naked man, humping Shelly from behind on the living room couch. As he'd guessed, she's completely passed out. The slices of bread hang limp between Gideon's lips as he watches half stupefied, half horrified. The man's testicles seem to slap Shelly's underside in rhythm to the music.

Wish my brain could throw up. I'd like to forget this... Gideon rushes out the front door and slams it so hard that it rattles the front windows.

Briskly walking through his upper middle class neighborhood, it occurs to him he's probably witnessed Shelly getting banged at least a hundred times. He wonders why she doesn't do it in her own room. Bitterly, he decides she probably has crabs in her bed.

He swallows his last bite of stale bread as he arrives at school.

GIDEON MEETS KAI

Natalie Brock scurries into the office. Fridays always seem so hectic. An adolescent she's never seen before seems miserably bored in the waiting area.

Another new student? Wonder who he's assigned to?

She smiles at him.

His face turns crimson, and he looks down at his shoes.

Another introvert, great...

She walks past him toward the supply closet.

Traci, the student administration aide, peeks over the filing cabinets.

"Hello, Mrs. Brock."

"Hi. Is that a new student?" Natalie tilts her head in the direction of the shy kid.

Bewildered, Traci asks, "Didn't you get the note I put in your mailbox last week?"

Natalie frowns. She's horrible at checking her mailbox ...unless of course it's Friday. They have donuts on Fridays.

Scanning the room for a pink pastry box, she asks, "What note?"

"The note Mr. Peterson had me type up informing you of an add-on. His name is Kai Tanaka. His transcripts are attached to the note."

"Is there anything I need to know about him? Any epilepsy, special needs, anything like that?"

Traci shakes her head. "No. He is bilingual though…fluent in Japanese."

Japanese? Natalie wonders how good his English is.

"Did his parents come in? Are they fluent in English?"

Traci rushes over.

As the teen starts to speak, Natalie stares at her incredibly thick braces. *There's a shortage of steel somewhere, thanks to Traci.*

"His dad came in. I think he's solo." The teen whispers, "Maybe his wife had an affair with a younger man. You know, the pool boy or the gardener…then they ran off with all his money, leaving him alone with just the kid."

Natalie giggles. "You teenagers and your wild imaginations." She catches sight of the pastry box next to the staff mail boxes.

"Donuts!"

She rushes over. After thoughtfully eyeballing each one, she selects a sugar-coated jelly, then sinks her teeth into it.

Devouring half, she sets it down, then licks her sticky fingers before pulling Kai's transcript from her mailbox. Admiring the delicate seal on the outside of the envelope she carefully removes the document.

Holy Cow. Kai's I.Q. is 146.

Glancing at her seating chart, she wonders where to put him. Then it dawns on her; she has another fifteen-year-old brainiac in her class, Gideon Damascus.

Every time she looks at him, he reminds her of Victor.

Natalie thinks back to her early twenties when she and her friends partied at Victor's house. *Every girl wanted to screw Victor Damascus.* To her knowledge, most of them did.

Victor was newly married but his wife was never around. Gone for months at a time, she did humanitarian work in third world countries.

Victor wasn't one to be lonely. The rich philanderer supplied Natalie and her friends with all sorts of drugs. He was tall, handsome, well-endowed, and able to go at it all night long.

Blushing, Natalie stuffs the remaining donut in her mouth.

Picking up her seating chart, she pencils Kai's name next to Gideon's.

Fifteen minutes later, Gideon wanders into his geography class. He is still in a foul mood and his head aches.

He looks across the room to discover he no longer enjoys the stigma of being the lone wolf in the back corner. There's a scrawny oriental kid sitting at the desk adjoined to his.

I knew it was too good to last forever. Like sitting on a plane next to an empty seat every day. No one's that lucky.

Kai sits hunkered down in his chair attempting to make himself invisible. Unnoticed, he watches two boys taking turns tossing spit balls at each other.

A tall kid approaches him.

"Hey," says Gideon as he takes a seat next to Kai.

Kai barely glances in his direction. "Hi," he says cheerlessly.

As the desks fill, students begin gawking at Kai as if he's a freak show. When they aren't rubbernecking, they're whispering amongst themselves. He assumes, about him.

Gideon notices Kai attempting to slink further down into his desk. He mutters quietly, "Don't mind them, they're all idiots."

As the teacher walks in, the room falls quiet.

"We have a new student joining us today. Everyone please say 'hello' to Kai Tanaka." Students turn to look at him. Kai meekly lifts his hand, waves, then sets it back down.

"Do you want to tell us where you came from, Kai?"

The entire class again turns to look at him. Blushing, he replies, "Japan."

"Which part?"

"Tokyo."

"Does anyone know what Tokyo is famous for?"

No one responds.

"Mount Fuji, which happens to be the highest volcano in Japan. In honor of our new student, please get out your geography books and turn to page eighty-six."

Students moan as they pull out their books. The buffoon along the wall who barely fits in his desk says loudly, "Thanks, dorkus."

Gideon hears Kai whisper under his breath, "Sorry."

He feels bad for Kai, but not as sorry as he feels for himself. He still can't get the gross image of the man in his living room out of his head.

As the hour passes, Gideon's thoughts are distracted by the city of Tokyo. Among other things, it's a leader in electronics, something he has a passion for.

When the bell rings, students begin to shuffle out. Kai stuffs his book in his backpack and looks up to find a small group of girls standing at his desk waiting to introduce themselves. Gideon observes as the marshmallow twinkie goes first.

"Hi, Kai, I'm Chantelle." She begins babbling.

Gideon gets up from his seat. He throws his backpack over his shoulder and hurries over so he can intentionally slam into the buffoon. The idiot had almost managed to get his fat ass out of his desk before Gideon knocks him back in. Having lived with Shelly, he's used to dealing with a bully. He leans over the fat kid and quietly asks, "Who's the dorkus now, asshole?"

Over the next two weeks, Gideon finds that sharing a desk isn't so bad after all. Being the smartest kid in school, other students resented him for messing up the curve. Now they hate Kai just as much.

Just before lunch, Gideon comes around the corner to find two bullies picking on Kai. He drops his backpack, grabs each of them by the scruff, then knocks their heads together. They fall to the ground. As one boy starts to get up, Gideon grabs his collar, then butts his head into a locker door. The kid falls back down.

Gideon glares at him. "Don't get up, stupid."

The other boy crawls away. He isn't going to chance getting his head bashed. Kids in the hallway gather around screaming, "Fight! Fight! Fight!" As teachers come running, students clear out like gas station cockroaches caught in the light.

After that, Gideon takes it upon himself to watch over Kai to make sure he doesn't get beat up. It isn't hard. The story of what happened traveled through school quickly and depending on who told it, it's highly exaggerated. Everyone is too afraid of Gideon to chance picking on Kai.

Little by little, Gideon discovers that he and Kai have a lot in common. They meet outside at lunch at the far end of the benches to commiserate over their home life.

"There's no way your dad is as bad as Shelly. The whole house smells like booze and B.O. She parties every night and it doesn't stop until she's passed out."

"That sucks," says Kai, "but at least you can come and go as you please."

Gideon sees Chantelle approaching from across the lawn.

"Dude, the twinkie's coming over."

Kai frowns at him. "Seriously, do you have to call her that?"

Chuckling, Gideon says, "I'll see ya later." In his opinion, aside from being a fat ass, Chantelle is intrusive and chatty. The thought of Kai swapping spit with her, grosses him out.

Just before summer break, Kai informs Gideon that his dad enrolled him in summer school.

"He only signed me up so he can work without worrying that I might get into trouble."

"He sounds like a total ass wipe. Can't you tell him you have a study session after class or something?"

Kai smiles, "You know, I think that might actually work. Classes get out at three, but he doesn't get home until six."

Every day after summer school, Kai meets Gideon at the video arcade. Gideon never has any money, but Kai never seems to mind paying for him.

TANAKA HOUSE

The half day schedule feels as though it's dragging at a snail's pace. The new semester brought with it a new history teacher, Osgood Smith. His thinning greasy strands of hair lie plastered into a wave across the top of his bald head. The dandruff in his unruly eyebrows seems to magnetically stick to his dirty glasses. Any flakes lucky enough to escape beyond that settle down onto his shoulders, hiding deep in the fibers of his polyester sportscoat. There's no telling how long it's been since the garment has seen soap and water.

Mr. Smith is mean. He enjoys doling out pointless exercises. Gideon refers to them as 'brain fucks.' A form of mind masturbation which clearly gives Mr. Smith some kind of sinister rise. Today is a brain fuck day.

In consideration of the half day schedule, Mr. Smith decides his class will perform an exercise in the momentum of time.

"We will all endure five minutes of silence."

Gideon's fuming about it. He, along with the whole class, quietly watch the clock.

Four minutes in, Mr. Smith creeps up beside Benjamin, who made the terrible mistake of nodding off. Mr. Smith slams a book down onto the corner of his desk.

Poor Bennie all but falls out of his seat.

After the five minute mark, students begin chatting. A loud crack startles the entire room. Everyone looks up to find that Mr. Smith has just slammed his ruler down onto his desk. By the sound of it, it may as well been a two by four.

"Silence!"

The remaining thirty minutes drag. In an unwavering monotone, Mr. Smith reads his favorite sections of *Mein Kampf* to the class. His love of misery, it seems, is endless.

When the bell rings, Mr. Smith waits at the door. He has students line up, letting them out one at a time.

Gideon purposely waits at the back of the line. He uses a tissue to steal a pen off Mr. Smith's desk, then quickly stuffs it into his backpack.

Kai waits out in the hall to gripe about what happened to Bennie.

"What a total bonehead," says Kai.

Gideon agrees. "I'm sure Mr. Smith gets his kicks out of being an asshole."

"He's a psycho sadistic freak. Someday we'll read about him in the papers and it won't be good."

Gideon doesn't doubt it.

As they reach the lockers, Kai asks, "Hey, dude, since it's a half day and all, do you want to come over to my house?"

Gideon grins. "Sure, thanks."

"Of course, you can't tell anyone. I'll have to sneak you in under the radar."

"Uh, remember, dude, you're my only friend. Who am I going to tell?"

"Good point. We can secretly hang out for a couple of hours before my father gets home."

Gideon grins. "Cool. Besides, he can't freak about something he doesn't know."

Kai nods in agreement. "I'll meet you at your locker after class."

As the morning drags on, Gideon wonders if Kai will chicken out. He often talks about how strict his dad is, as if he's afraid of him.

Shortly after the final bell, Gideon finds Kai waiting for him by his locker.

"Do you need to call your mom to let her know you're coming over?"

"She's not my mom, she's my foul 'stepmother.' An evil one at that." Gideon tosses his books in his locker adding, "She couldn't give a crap where I'm at."

The boys stroll out to the school parking lot.

Gideon lowers his voice, "Dude, check it out, it's a Bentley. Who do you suppose the lucky rich asshole is?"

Kai walks right up to the Bentley's impeccably dressed chauffeur.

Standing at attention, the chauffeur says, "Hello, Mr. Tanaka."

"Hi, Keiichi. Can you drop us off half a block from the house? We'll walk from there."

Gideon's mouth falls open.

"Of course, sir."

Kai slides in. He glances at Gideon, who's just standing there staring.

"Dude, are you coming or what?"

"Uh…uh huh."

As Gideon slides into the back seat, the smell of clean musk and Italian leather fills his senses. It reminds him of his dad's 1961 vintage Jaguar which is still parked in the garage at home.

Kai pushes a button on a panel in front of him. A window rises between them and the driver. He points to the glass. "He can't hear us now."

Gideon looks at him, astonished.

Bewildered, Kai asks, "What? What's wrong?"

"Why didn't you tell me you own a Bentley and have a butler?"

"We don't have a butler. Oh, you mean Keiichi?"

Gideon rolls his eyes. "Uh, yeah."

"He's our driver. And anyway, dude, you're lucky that you get to walk home and basically do anything you want. Me, I'm a prisoner. My father has me watched constantly like a baby."

"What do you mean?"

Kai frowns. "He doesn't let me out of his sight. I can barely take a piss without him looking over my shoulder."

"Dude, that sucks." Gideon searches for something to say to make him feel better. "At least it proves he cares about you."

"It only proves he's a control freak. He doesn't do stuff like other fathers do. He doesn't fish, go to movies or baseball games or anything like that. He always says he's too busy and I doubt he'd even like that stuff."

Kai throws himself back in his seat, pouting.

"What stuff does he like?"

"Nothing, he just works."

"There has to be something. Does he have a hobby or collect anything?"

Kai thinks about it for a moment.

"Well, kind of a hobby, yeah, I guess you'd call it that."

"Kind of a hobby?"

"It would be easier to show you, but you can't tell anyone."

Gideon laughs. "Why? Does he make drugs or something?"

Kai sits up in his seat to face Gideon. "I'm serious. You have to promise because if you told anyone, I'd get in a lot of trouble and we wouldn't be able to hang out anymore."

"Wow, dude, you're joking, right?" Gideon studies Kai's face. "I can't tell if you're messing with me or not."

"It's not that I wouldn't want to hang out with you, but the police would show up at my house. I wouldn't be *able* to hang out with you."

Gideon raises an eyebrow.

The car stops. Kai says, "Wait for Keiichi. He'll open the door for us."

Both boys get out and watch the car pull away. They stroll up the road in the same direction.

"Sorry, Kai. I didn't grasp the seriousness of this. What do you need me to do or say, or not do or not say?"

"Okay, see, it's like this. My father has, uh, these special pets. The thing is, they're illegal here in the U.S., so I've got to have your word you won't tell anyone."

Gideon halts, then puts his right hand over his chest and holds up his left hand. "I promise, dude. I won't tell anyone about your dad's pets. Not one word."

Kai stares, then teasingly slaps Gideon on the arm. "You moron. You're supposed to raise your right hand."

"Oh, right." Gideon switches hands. "I promise."

"Yeah, okay."

As they meander up the street, Gideon asks, "So these pets, do they do tricks?"

Kai laughs. "Uh, yeah, they do."

As they approach Kai's residence, Gideon sees armed security guards in a small building alongside the front gate.

He mumbles, "Seriously, you live in a fortress? Dude, when were you going to tell me about this!?"

Kai shrugs apologetically. A guard sticks his head out of the guard station.

"Hello, Mr. Tanaka."

"Hi." Kai waves his hand sheepishly.

He and Gideon climb into a black golf cart. A guard hops into the driver's seat. Gideon's eyes flicker at the bars of light cascading through the trees as the cart makes it's way up the long driveway.

"How big is this property?"

Kai shrugs. "I don't know."

Halfway up the drive, Gideon gazes at the immense cherry blossom trees on each side of the pavement. They stand like soldiers, shoulder to shoulder as the thickly flowered branches intertwine arm in arm with their comrades. Petals sporadically fall beneath them in the shadows.

When they reach the top, there's a glass guard tower. Gideon sees an AK-47 propped up against the thick transparent wall. The holes drilled here and there are indicative of bullet proof glass.

The cart guard waves up to the tower guard. He nods, allowing them access to the massive mansion a hundred yards ahead.

"Dude, this place is awesome!"

"Wait till you see inside."

Kai tells the guard to stop the cart. "We can walk from here, thanks."

As they begin walking up the remainder of the path, Gideon glances at the rooftop. It tilts up at each corner, emphasizing the oriental architecture. Huge tropical plants frame the tinted windows. Tall wooden beams support the verandas that wrap around the full length of the mansion.

Gideon notices there are cameras all around. He wonders if Kai's dad is some kind of drug lord.

27

Sixty yards in, they come to two ten-foot dragons sitting on either side of a bamboo covered walkway that extends over water.

"Whoa, cool!"

As they walk along the passage, Gideon marvels at the koi ponds on either side of it.

When they finally reach the front door, Gideon is awestruck by a waterfall coming off the top of the building.

Kai enters a code on the key pad on the door. An electronic hum follows, unlatching the bolt inside.

He politely waits for Gideon to enter first.

Distracted by the school of small blue fish swimming in the base of the waterfall, Gideon swirls his finger in the water.

"Dude, c'mon already!"

As soon as they enter the house, Kai quickly shuts the door. He makes a fist, pumping it up and down in mid-air, chanting "Yesss! Yesss! Yesss!"

Confused, Gideon asks, "What's with the lame nerd freak fist pump?"

"I didn't know if I could get you in! The guards are supposed to keep everyone out." Kai grins proudly, adding, "You're the first friend I've ever had over."

"Man, it would suck to live like that." As he says it, Gideon realizes he's never had anyone over either.

Kai rolls his eyes. "It's imprisonment."

As they walk through the entrance hall, Gideon's mouth falls open. The hall overlooking the white sunken living room seems large enough to comfortably store a small airplane. A glass wall overlooks the Tanaka's beautiful back yard.

Winding through the middle of the room is an actual creek with green grass and miniature bamboo. The sound of trickling water is wonderful.

"Where's the water coming from?"

Kai points to the bamboo shoots protruding through a wall, supplying water to the creek.

"It's pumped in from a fresh spring on our property. It gets circulated through filters that kill any algae."

"It's amazing."

"My father has this thing about living with nature as much as humanly possible. We still have a guy that comes every week, though, to check on the koi and test the water."

As they move into the middle of the room, Gideon spots an orange flash in the creek. His eyes follow it underneath the glass wall to the pond outside.

"The koi are pretty shy. Sometimes they'll let you pet them if you have food."

"This place is so cool."

"I guess." Kai shrugs. "It's just where I live."

"Where I live," Gideon laments, "it's a dirty hellhole. The whole house smells like booze and dirty socks."

Kai clears his throat uncomfortably.

Staring through the huge panes of infinity glass, Gideon admires the tall white eucalyptus trees in the back yard.

"What's that platform for?" he asks, pointing to a landing high up in the tallest tree.

"The gardeners use it to trim the trees."

"Have you climbed up there?"

Kai rolls his eyes. "What, are you nuts?!"

"Afraid of heights, huh? I'd love to sit up there with a peanut butter and jelly sandwich." His eyes travel down to the base of the tree.

"Hey, what's that?" He points to the black mass.

"That's Koko, our poodle bijon." Kai frowns. "He has a bad leg so he sleeps in the shade a lot."

"Did he get hit by a car or something?"

Kai lowers his head. "My father accidentally kicked him. That is, he says it was an accident, but…he has no patience for anything."

"Is he some kind of dog hater?"

"No. He's just mean."

Wanting to change the subject Kai asks, "Hey, want to check out my video game room?"

Gideon's face lights up. "You have a game room?"

Kai motions for Gideon to follow him. They head down the hall and stop at a large black door. Gideon gazes at the carvings in the wood depicting dragons and warriors in battle.

Pushing the door open, Kai waves Gideon inside. "C'mon, check it out."

As Gideon's eyes adjust to the darkness, he's delighted by what he sees.

"Hey, dude, you know what you were saying about being a prisoner?"

"Yeah."

"I want to be a prisoner, too."

Gideon mimics Kai's nerd freak fist pump. "You never told me you have a fucking game room!"

Kai laughs, "Oh my god, you're right. That is lame."

"Told ya."

"And now..." Kai waves Gideon further into the room, gesturing him toward the four video game chairs facing a huge flat screen and cabinets loaded to capacity with video games. On the other side of the room are a dozen arcade games, including three video game booths. They walk through an archway leading to an adjoining room with a pool table. To the right is a long, highly polished black bar, with a mirror behind it. The edges glow in purple neon. Gideon looks at the various bottles of booze. There's every kind of alcohol imaginable. *This would be Shelly's wet dream.*

At the very back of the room is another archway leading to a small theater. Gideon gazes at the huge open skylight.

"Dude, you have four floors here?"

"Yep."

Gideon walks over to one of the leather chairs and hops into it. On the right arm of the chair is a panel of buttons.

"What do all these buttons do?"

31

Kai pushes two of them. The skylight closes, Gideon's chair reclines, and a large screen drops from the ceiling.

"It's just where we watch movies."

"Wow, that's so cool. What kind of screen is it? Plasma? L.E.D?"

"No idea. That's too sciencey for me. I just know what buttons to push. C'mon, let's play some games."

They go back to the gaming area. Gideon sticks his head into one of the flight booths.

"Hey, these are just like real cockpits." He hops into the seat.

"Actually, they are real cockpits. My father got them from the military. Most cockpits have one game, but this can play up to twenty games."

Gideon grabs the joystick and starts pushing buttons.

Kai laughs. "Press star and the down button."

"Hello, Master."

Gideon glances toward the female voice and sees two Japanese women entering the room.

"Hi," says Kai. He looks over at Gideon to see his reaction.

As he realizes what they are wearing, Gideon hops out of the cockpit.

Both women are carrying trays, wearing nothing but white aprons and black stilettos. They turn their backs to the boys to set the trays down. Large starched bows cover their buttocks. As if they had read Gideon's mind, both trays are stocked with peanut butter and jelly sandwiches. There are chips, chocolate cookies, and flavored bottled water.

Both women kneel in front of Kai.

The taller girl asks, "Will that be all, sir?"

Kai turns to Gideon, "Uh, I don't know. Will that be all, Gideon?"

Speechless, with a stupefied look on his face, Gideon continues to stare. Kai knuckles him in the ribs.

"Uh, uh huh."

"Yes, Houseki, thank you. Thank you, Oishii."

The girls put their hands together, bow, and back away. They giggle as they leave the room.

"Oh my God, dude! I saw their butts! They're naked! Do they always walk around like that? Who are they?"

"Those are father's special pets."

"But, wait, I thought," Gideon stammers. "The koi fish, aren't they--?"

Kai laughs. "You thought the koi were his pets?"

"You mean, those girls, those hot naked girls, are your dad's pets?"

"Uh huh."

Kai plops himself down in front of the food. Gideon sits next to him.

"Grown women as pets? I didn't know there was such a thing."

"Remember, you can't tell anyone."

Gideon nods. "I'd like to make a pet out of my stepmother. I'd put a dog collar on her and beat the crap out of her. I don't want to see her naked butt, though. I see it enough as it is when she's passed out."

Kai hands Gideon a sandwich. "Dude, that's messed up. C'mon, eat, I'll introduce you to them later."

Gideon's voice squeaks, "Introduce me?"

"Yeah, don't you want to talk to them?"

Gideon's eyes grow wide. He shoves his sandwich in his mouth, chewing fast.

"Hey, slow down, you'll give yourself a stomach ache."

Gideon swallows. "Oh man, we have to convince your dad to let me come over and hang out. We got to get on his good side."

"I don't think he has a good side. If he knew you were here, he'd freak."

"Too bad he's an asshole. Hey, maybe we should introduce him to my stepmother. Just think. We could be brothers and hang out all the time."

Kai always wanted a brother. His eyes wander to the ceiling as he pictures it in his mind. "One big twisted family."

Gideon shakes his head. "Nah, forget it, dude. You're too cool. I couldn't do that to you. Actually, I'd never wish that gold digging bitch on anyone, even your dad. Besides, she'd probably turn him in."

"That would not be good."

"Yeah, or she'd blackmail him if she thought she could get money out of it."

"She should be shot."

Gideon practically chokes. "Aw, shit! Since when do you say stuff like that? I'm a bad influence."

Kai laughs. "I'm just joking. I don't really want her shot."

Gideon takes a swig of his drink, then sets it down. "You may be joking, but I've been thinking about ways to kill her for years."

"You know that would make you a real psycho, right?"

Gideon nods. "Then I'm a psycho because someday, I *am* going to kill her."

"Seriously, Gideon. You don't really want to kill her, do you?"

"If it wasn't for her, my dad would still be alive. So yeah, dude, I think about killing her nasty ass every day."

Troubled by Gideon's horrible predicament, Kai says, "Sorry about your father."

"Me too. Thanks, though." Gideon holds up a potatoe chip. "These are so good! I never get food like this."

"Houseki makes them from scratch. My father has this thing about always eating organic whenever possible."

"You're lucky you have food. Shelly buys bread sometimes. That's it."

Curious, Kai says, "Hey, I hope you don't mind me asking, what did your real parents do?"

"My pop was an electronics engineer. My mom was a biological chemist. My dad used to say if there was an epidemic, or they wanted to create one, they'd call my mother."

"You said, 'they.' They who?"

Gideon shrugs. "I asked the same thing. He said he wasn't allowed to say."

"That's weird."

Crunching a chip, Gideon adds, "My mom read to me a lot and she loved to play toesies."

"What's toesies?"

"She'd paint little faces on both of our toes. She'd tell me all their names. If I couldn't remember a name, she'd wipe the face off. Depending on how many faces I got right, that's how many animal crackers I'd get. It taught me how to remember names and faces."

Kai pictures it in his mind. "She sounds nice. It must have been hard losing her."

"Not half as hard as being stuck with Shelly. It's like we have a revolving door in our house for any asshole looking for sex."

"What about your mom?" Gideon asks. "I've never heard you talk about her."

"She died in childbirth. I never knew her."

"That sucks. Sorry you got stuck with your psycho dad."

Kai laughs. "What are the chances I'd know two psycho's? You and my father."

Gideon chuckles, "Okay, so lesson number one. If you want to get on your dad's good side, ask him how his day went."

"Really?"

Gideon helps himself to another cookie.

"Uh huh. I learned that from my dad's attorney. He knows I hate my stepmother. Mr. Spencer said it would help Shelly be nicer to me."

"Did it work?"

"Yeah, it actually did for a while. But I got so tired of her shit that I just couldn't fake how much I hated her anymore."

"I'll try it. Hey, dude, did I tell you we have a pool? I can show it to you later if you like."

"Sure. Let's play video games first."

They finish lunch, then delve into the games.

An hour later, Kai looks at his watch.

"C'mon, dude, I want to show you the pool before you go."

Kai leads Gideon up three flights of stairs, then across a glass, water-filled catwalk. They stop for a moment to watch the fish swim through it, underneath their feet.

Gideon can hardly believe how cool Kai's house is. "Seriously, dude, this is the most amazing place I've ever seen."

When they get to the pool, Gideon is awestruck. A giant stone statue of a dragon sleeps in the sun at one corner of the pool.

Kai reaches down to feel the water. "You should come over to swim sometime."

"You don't have to twist my arm." Gideon slowly strolls around the pool. The corners are shaped into lotus flowers. By his estimation, the pool is at least fifty feet long. A basin runs along the far edge on the opposite side. He walks over to investigate. It's filled with the same blue fish he saw at the front door.

Kai glances at his watch again and waves Gideon back to the statue where he's standing. "Dude, c'mon, we don't have much time."

As Gideon walks toward him, he notices an iridescence in the stone.

"What kind of stone is that?"

"Labradorite. It's thousands of years old."

"Where did it come from?"

"Japan. It belonged to some emperor, back in the ninth century. It was part of my grandfather's art collection. He collected art all over the world."

"You never mention him. What's your grandfather like?"

Sadly, Kai replies, "I don't know. He died in a car accident when I was little. My father doesn't like to talk about him much."

Kai leads Gideon to the far end of the pool. It extends past the edge of the building, overlooking tropical gardens and ponds.

"They call this an infinity pool. It's an illusion that makes the water seem as though it's flowing right outside and over the edge."

"Where does the water go?"

"There's a basin just beyond the wall. It's piped around the house to supply water to the waterfalls at the front door."

Gideon pictures it in his head. "And it gets circulated back up to the pool?"

"Yep, exactly."

"Is the water warm?" Gideon bends down to put his hand in the pool. It's tepid. He glances up at Kai, smiling.

"Nice, right?"

Gideon nods. "How do you keep the fish alive what with clorine and all?"

"The pool's filled with salt water. It doesn't need clorine."

"Really? Cool."

Kai checks his watch again. "I've got to kick you out before my father gets home."

They head downstairs. Kai calls the guard on the intercom to come back up. As they reach the door, Gideon says, "Too bad I didn't get to talk to your dad's pets."

"There's always tomorrow." Kai winks.

Gideon's face lights up.

"I think we'll be okay so long as we watch the time and limit it to two hours."

"That's awesome, dude!"

Walking out the front door, Gideon sees the guard waiting for him at the end of the walkway.

He turns toward Kai. "Hey, how rich is your dad anyway?"

"I don't know. Pretty rich I suppose. I mean how many people have people as pets?"

That evening, Gideon sets his alarm to wake up two hours before sunrise.

He rises at four a.m., then dresses in a black hoodie, black sweat pants, and black leather gloves. When he reaches Mr. Smith's cul-de-sac, he sees a little terrier running around in the street. The dog watches him but doesn't approach. Gideon's thankful he's not a yapper.

He crouches down beside Mr. Smith's car and uses his switchblade to let all the air out of his left tires. As he creeps around to the other side of the vehicle, he sees the little dog taking a shit on Mr. Smith's front lawn.

Grinning, he gives the dog a thumbs up. He lets the air out of the two right tires. Pulling the note from his pocket, he re-reads it:

Five minutes of silence is indeed a long time out of one's life. About as long as it takes to bleed to death.

He tucks the note under Mr. Smith's front tire.

Half way down the cul-de-sac he looks back. The dog's small silhouette in the middle of the street tells Gideon he's watching him. He lets out one short quick whistle. The dog bolts toward him. Within seconds, it's at

40

his feet, panting and wagging its tail. Gideon leans over and lets the dog smell his hand. It sniffs him, then tucks its head under his fingers. After a few minutes of petting, Gideon checks the collar. "Flash." It suits him.

"Good boy, Flash. Now stay."

The dog watches him make his way down the street but doesn't follow him.

He's one smart dog.

GIDEON'S LIST

Mid-Saturday, Gideon lazily lies in bed thinking up ideas to add to his "100 Ways to Kill A House Pest" list. He's fairly certain when he reaches a hundred, he'll have figured out how best to exterminate Shelly. He pulls the crinkled list from in between his mattress and box spring to review it:

In-Home Accidents: Included among them; death due to fire, asphyxiation, and a bathtub drowning. After reading it, he decides the last doesn't seem too feasible. Everything he's ever researched about an adult drowning in a tub usually ends with an indictment.

Poisoning: In order to get away with poisoning, it needs to dissipate quickly so that it won't be detected in an autopsy. As Gideon looks up the list of candidate poisons, it occurs to him, a simple hefty dose of potassium chloride directly into the blood stream might do the trick. It would be simple enough to inject if Shelly's passed out, which in her case, is a no-brainer. Being that potassium and chloride are already present in the body, any trace of it may not seem all that unusual. He puts a star next to it.

Stabbing: After perusing his list of splendid stabbing ideas, it occurs to him he'd have to clean up the mess. That being the case, he'd need to stab her somewhere away from the house. It would take some planning.

Yard Accidents: All of the ideas in this section involve dragging Shelly's passed out body into the yard. There's the tree limb impalement, rebar impalement, and leaving her plastered lazy carcass in the middle of the street. If he smashes out the street lamp and covers her with a dark blanket, she'd almost certainly get run over. This idea seems totally feasible to him so he puts a star next to it.

Hitman: Not knowing anyone in the assassination business, he'd probably have to hire one of Shelly's deadbeat boyfriends. Chances are, any one of them would do it, but he couldn't be sure if they would blab about it.

"Gideon!"

Grimacing, he rises out of bed. He shoves the list inside his carved-out edition of *War and Peace*. He seriously doubts Shelly can read, let alone want to pick up a book without pictures.

He opens his bedroom door and looks over the bannister.

"Gideon!"

"I'm right here, Shelly. You can stop yelling." *God, she's so drunk she can hardly stand up.*

On the bottom stair, Shelly holds the railing with one hand and a half-gallon bottle of vodka with the other. Wearing a dirty see-through baby doll with matching panties, she stares at up at his bare chest and licks her lips.

Gross.

"My, look at you. How you've grown." She lets go of the bannister to twirl her overly dry bleached out hair. "Maybe we should hang out sometime."

He's surprised she noticed. He's grown almost six inches in the last six months. He's the tallest kid in his grade. Had it not been for Kai insisting he come along to buy school clothes, he'd be wearing high waters.

He watches her take a huge swig from her half-gallon bottle.

Her eyes meander down his body again, stopping at his boxers. She stares at his package as if it's a jack-in-the-box.

Disgusted, Gideon asks, "What do you need?"

"Oh, you know what I need." She laughs at herself for teasing him.

Gideon turns away to head back to his room.

Shelly yells, "Gideon, don't you dare walk away from me when I'm talking to you!"

Heat rises in his face as he turns and heads back to the bannister. He shouts angrily, "Then tell me what the fuck you want, Shelly!"

She's taken aback. She can't remember Gideon ever yelling at her. Narrowing her eyes at him, she says, "I'm having a party tonight. Stay upstairs. Read, jerk off, or whatever it is that you do up there."

Annoyed, he says coldly, "Fine." Gideon heads back into his room and slams the door behind him. His head begins to throb as he pulls *War and Peace* off his book case. Unfolding the list he scribbles in caps: FUCK HER TO DEATH WITHOUT TOUCHING HER.

POOL PARTY

It takes an effort for Gideon to convince himself that turning sixteen is just another day. It would come and go like any other year, unnoticed. When he thinks of all the shit he's been through, and still managed to survive, it's a milestone. Having never received balloons, cards or gifts since his parents died, any kind of acknowledgement would've been astonishing. Gideon leaves the house in the same way that he does every weekday, with plain sliced bread and the image of his stepmother passed out on the couch.

Arriving at his locker, he retrieves his book for class, then turns toward the hall to find Kai standing behind him.

"Happy birthday." Kai holds out a wrapped gift.

Gideon looks at the shitty wrapping job and smiles.

"Thanks, dude. How'd you know?"

"I got it from metal mouth in the front office. She gave it to me a few months ago. Go ahead, open it."

Tearing off the paper, Gideon sees it's a video game.

"Wow, Death Brigade Three?! I can't wait to play it!"

He flips it over to read the back of the box.

Kai beams, proud of himself for choosing the right gift. "We've got a big day ahead, Oishii is making you a cake. Houseki is going to bar-b-que. We can play Death Brigade until lunchtime and then hang out at the pool all afternoon."

Gideon gives him a questioning look. "Are you suggesting we cut?"

Kai rolls his eyes. "No one goes to school on their birthday. It's supposed to be anti-religious or something. C'mon, Keiichi is waiting in the parking lot."

Gideon tosses his books back into his locker and slams it shut.

As they cross the parking lot, Gideon asks, "So, how is it that we're not going to get in trouble?"

"Oishii will write you an excuse. She forges my father's signature every year on my birthday."

When they arrive at the Tanaka house, the boys spend all morning in the game room. The graphics on Gideon's new game are epic, just like the reviews promised.

Just before noon, Houseki calls on the intercom. "We're ready for you at the pool."

Kai answers. "We're just going to change and we'll be right up."

He loans Gideon a pair of swimming trunks.

Not wanting to be a bummer by mentioning he can't swim, Gideon decides he'll just stay in the shallow end.

When they step outside the glass doors to the pool, the heavenly scent of bar-b-que makes Gideon's mouth water.

"Man, that smells delicious."

In unison, the girls chant, "Happy birthday, Gideon!"

He smiles at them and glances at Koko. The dog is planted at Houseki's feet, hoping she'll drop something.

The girls made beef ribs, chicken, potato salad and garlic bread.

Grateful, Gideon says, "This is the best birthday party ever."

He turns to Kai, "Actually, it's the only birthday party ever."

Kai frowns. "Didn't your stepmom ever give you a cake or a party for your birthday?"

Gideon laughs. "Are you kidding?! Shelly's barely sober enough to figure out what day of the week it is."

"Dude, that's messed up."

Kai turns to Houseki and Oishii. "Will you girls join us for lunch? You did all this work so you should eat too."

As they all sit down at the table, it occurs to Gideon that Kai, Oishii, and Houseki are like family to him. Oishii makes peanut butter sandwiches whenever he comes over, and Houseki always packs a batch of cookies for him to take home.

He glances over at Houseki. She blushes and looks down at her plate.

What was that? He wonders if she knows he likes her.

After lunch, Gideon gets up and pulls off his shirt.

They all tease him about his farmer tan.

"You need to put on sunscreen so your skin doesn't burn," says Houseki. She brings over a tube of sun screen and begins applying it to his back.

She takes her time, moving to his neck, chest and arms.

The feeling of her hands on him is nice.

47

By the time she's done, Gideon's hard. Embarrassed, he sits with his hands in his lap for several minutes before getting up.

Oishii sits down next to Kai to apply sunscreen to his back and chest. "Take off your shirt."

"No, I'll swim with my shirt on. I'm not taking it off."

After a heated discussion, he allows her to apply sunscreen to the back of his neck, arms, and legs.

The girls head downstairs with the dishes. Gideon walks over to the steps at the shallow end of the pool.

"We should wait a bit before swimming," says Kai. "Otherwise we'll get a stomach ache."

"Oh, okay." Gideon walks over to the jacuzzi and stands on the first step. Despite the excessive heat, it feels amazing. After a minute, he sinks down into the water until it's up to his chin.

Kai slips into the hot tub, opposite him. "Ah, this is the life, isn't it?"

Gideon nods. "If I could, I'd sit in here every day."

Wearing sun glasses and black thong bikinis, Oishii and Houseki return to the pool.

The boys grin at each other and watch as the girls apply coconut oil to each other.

Hearing them giggle periodically, Gideon slides over next to Kai. "They know we're watching them."

Houseki gets up to straighten her towel, which is already laid out perfectly. She bends over with her ass pointed directly at them.

"God, how I'd love to bend her over like that," mumbles Gideon.

Kai laughs. "Me too."

Gideon tries to find any kind of a flaw. Each girl's arms and legs match perfectly. Neither one has an ounce of extra fat.

"Those girls make us look fat, and we're skinny," says Kai.

Grinning, Gideon asks, "Which one would you choose if you could have sex with them?"

"Oishii. She's shorter."

"Have you ever thought about asking them for sex?"

Kai blushes. "All the time, but I'm afraid they'd tell my father."

Sniggering, Gideon says, "They won't tell your dad. They'd get into just as much trouble as you."

It occurs to Kai, Gideon's probably right.

Kai rises from the jacuzzi. "It's hot, let's cool off in the pool."

"Okay."

Kai dives in, splashing the girls.

"Hey!" shouts Houseki. "You're getting us wet!"

Gideon smiles salaciously at her as he walks over to the pool steps. *Yeah, wet.*

Houseki leans over to whisper something to Oishii. Both girls get up and leave the pool area.

Confused, Gideon asks, "Why'd they leave? "Did splashing them piss them off?"

"Nah. It'd take a lot more than that. They're probably just going to get your birthday cake."

Gideon descends down into the cool water. "Hey, I was wondering...do they basically have to do anything you say?"

Kai thinks about it. "Maybe. Actually, I don't know."

"Can we test it out when they bring up the cake?"

Kai grins, "Yeah, let's. You do it."

It crosses Gideon's mind, Kai's been trying to make out with the twinkie, when all this time he could have been banging his hot servants instead.

The elevator door dings. The girls wheel out a cart with a chocolate cake with lit candles. Everyone sings, "Happy Birthday."

Lifting the cake, Houseki carries it over to Gideon.

"Make a wish."

He grins at her and closes his eyes. Taking a deep breath, he blows out all of the candles.

As the girls begin cutting the cake, Gideon looks over at Kai and tilts his head toward the jacuzzi.

They both rush back to the hot tub.

The girls each carry a slice of chocolate cake over.

"You girls should join us," says Kai.

The boys watch as they saunter to the cake to get a piece for themselves, then make their way back to the jacuzzi.

Deciding this is his best chance to make a move on Houseki, Gideon slides over to allow her to sit next to him. Oishii sits across from them next to Kai.

Gideon takes a bite of cake. It's delicious. He turns to Houseki. "Do you have to do everything Kai asks?"

"For the most part, yes. We just can't do anything that would cause harm to him or us."

Gideon glances at Kai and raises and lowers his eyebrows.

Kai laughs nervously.

Gideon turns to face Houseki again. He sets his plate on the edge of the jacuzzi. His adrenaline spikes as he says, "The frosting is delicious. Definitely worth sharing." He scoops up a blob and spreads it across her chest.

Oishii and Kai laugh.

Houseki looks down at the chocolate mess, then looks up smiling at him.

Gideon turns to Kai, asking nervously. "Hey, dude, uh, would if be okay if I clean that up for her?"

Kai speaks to Houseki in Japanese. She reaches behind her neck and unties the string to her bikini top. It falls down, exposing her bare breasts.

Houseki's eyes sparkle at Gideon as he moves around the step to get directly in front of her. He admires her breasts, which are round and perky. Her pretty pink nipples poke out at him like small gumdrops.

Placing his hands on the step on either side of her, he takes his time licking and sucking the frosting off her skin. When he looks up, his face is covered in chocolate.

Houseki laughs and asks, "Is that what you wished for?"

"Not quite," he says, blushing.

He backs up, pulling her down into the water, barely aware that Kai and Oishii are exiting the jacuzzi.

Facing her, Gideon looks down into the water and runs his hands over her hips. Her skin feels silky. When he looks at her face she's smiling at him. She slowly reaches around her back to untie the bottom string to her bikini top. The garment falls into the water.

Taking hold of the side bows of her bikini bottom, Gideon pulls her toward him. He hesitates, watching the tips of her hair floating like black smoke around her in the water.

With his heart pounding in his chest, he tugs on her bows, wondering, *will she let me take them off?*

Houseki pulls him closer.

"Do it, Gideon."

He pulls on the bows, untying them, then tugs the garment away from her. His hands move to her soft round buttocks as he pulls her into him.

As she plants a tender kiss on his lips, he feels Houseki's hands sliding down his body. By the time she gets to his waistband, his cock is protruding past it.

She smiles and backs up slightly. "Take your trunks off."

Is this is really happening?!

Without hesitation, Gideon quickly yanks off his trunks. He tosses them up on the edge of the jacuzzi, then reaches for her.

She maneuvers herself over him, then slowly slides down onto him.

Gideon moans. He grabs firmly onto Houseki's hips. His face is tense as he begins to thrust. His body's sensations consume him as the water thrashes violently around them.

Houseki moans. Her body clamps down, throbbing all around Gideon's cock.

A surge of pleasure rises up, violently ripping through his core, causing his muscles to spasm with overwhelming gratification.

When it's over, Gideon opens his eyes. He looks at his surroundings.

Houseki laughs. "Now did you get what you wished for?"

Nodding, Gideon laughs. "Best birthday ever." He hands her her bikini.

Houseki puts it on and exits the jacuzzi.

Gideon looks around, wondering where Kai and Oishii disappeared to. He spots Kai sitting on the pool steps. Wedged between his legs is Oishii. Her face is in his lap.

A few days later, Gideon steals sixty dollars from Shelly's food money box so he can fill Kai's locker full of individually wrapped twinkies. It's his way of saying 'thanks' for his birthday bar-b-que.

Gideon arranges to leave class ten minutes early before students are let out for lunch. He stacks fifty cream filled cakes inside Kai's locker. Just as they start to wobble, he manages to get the locker door shut. He stands forty feet away at the water cooler to observe.

When the bell rings, the hallway quickly packs with students. Kai arrives at his locker, opens the door, and three-quarters of the crème filled cakes come tumbling out onto the floor. Nearby students quickly scramble to the floor to grab them up. Unabashed, they reach for the cakes in his locker. Kai manages to hang onto two of them for himself.

Gideon walks over to find Kai grinning broadly.

"Those are supposed to have a shelf life of something like a hundred years."

"Dude, you're the best." Kai rips open a package and stuffs the goo filled cake in his mouth.

THE SLEEPOVER

The cold fall air quickly leads to the school doors being shut. The foul reek of sweat and B.O. lingers in the hall. Gideon recognizes it as the distinct stench of testosterone. As he turns the corner, members of the football team attempt to solicit students into attending the football game.

After attending a game a month ago, Gideon is no longer keen on going. There are far too many guys looking for a fight and too many girls looking for adulation. Drunk girls at that, all hanging out with their respective stuck up cliques.

As he watches two jocks pummel each other to the ground, he thinks back to the last game he attended. He sat in the shadows at the back of the bleachers. He was there to observe the onlookers. The game was of no interest to him.

By the end of the night, he learned that loyalty only goes so far with the cliques. Make the mistake of getting puking drunk, and the flock quickly disenfranchises its member. Take little Ursula. It didn't matter who encouraged her to drink that night. They abandoned her for fear she'd puke in the car. She stood amongst the decaying leaves in the cold dark parking lot, watching her friends drive away without her. No one took responsibility for her, and later, no one took any of the blame for what happened to her. Gideon switches out his books, then turns to see the football players punching each other as they meander down the hall.

He glances at the wet dirty streaks of sweat all over the floor.

His mind flashes to the beads of sweat on the back of his hands as they wrapped around Ursula's tiny neck. *Poor terrified little Ursula.* She stood frozen in fear as he took her from behind. *It was a gift, her passing out.* She never saw him so he didn't have to bludgeon her. The attack was trouble-free, but it was risky.

From then on, he decided not to be so quick to take advantage of an easy opportunity. He'd choose the recipients of his attention very carefully.

His thoughts are interrupted when he sees Kai walking toward him.

"Hey Gid, we're still on, right? You're coming?"

"Yeah, I'm always coming," he says, grinning.

"That's gay, dude. Your idea of comedy is tragic."

"Speaking of tragic, I've been meaning to ask you. How's it going on the home front? With your dad I mean."

"We don't do anything together, but we talk more. I ask him about his day and he gives me the boring details."

"Well, I'm just wondering…I've been coming over for what, almost a year and a half now, right?"

Kai nods. "Sounds about right."

"And we've been fooling around with your servants for what, eight months or more?"

Kai looks up, attempting to recall how long it's actually been. "I guess so. What's your point?"

"Don't you think it's strange after all this time, we haven't been caught? I mean, isn't it weird no one's ever ratted us out?"

"Dude, I seriously doubt he knows. If so, why am I still breathing? Why are you still breathing?"

Alarmed, Gideon asks, "You don't seriously think he'd kill us or anything if he finds out, do you?"

"Uh, yeah. Think about it dude, we're fucking the same pussy he is."

"Aw, damn," Gideon frowns. "Why'd you have to put it that way? That grosses me out."

"Sorry, dude, I mean pets. To him, his pets are his possessions. You know, like gym equipment."

"He'd kill us for using his gym equipment?"

Kai shrugs. "It's my father, so depending on his mood…"

"C'mon, dude, this is serious!"

Kai realizes Gideon really is obsessing over it.

"Okay, let's look at this logically. Chances are if he knew, we wouldn't have any balls left."

Sarcastically, Gideon says, "That's supposed to make me feel better?!"

Kai glances at his watch. "Aw, man. I'm going to be late for class. Can we talk about it later?"

Gideon grumbles, "Yeah, later, dude."

As school gets out, Gideon and Kai meet up at the parking lot. The Bentley is double parked. Keiichi stands alongside it, unfazed by the line of parents glaring as they take turns squeezing past to get by.

Once the boys are in the back seat, Kai raises the divider so they can't be heard.

Gideon senses something's bothering him.

"Hey, it's cool if you don't want to hang out."

"I just got a lot on my mind. That's all."

"Uh huh…" says Gideon suspiciously. "And you can't tell me?"

"It's personal between me and Chantelle."

"Oh wait, don't tell me, let me guess, she still won't put out?"

Kai looks down at the floorboard and shakes his head.

"You're still just feeling her tits? For God's sake, just take her! I keep telling you she wants it. Every girl wants it. They just pretend they don't."

Kai frowns. "You don't know her like I do. Anyway, I disagree with you. They don't all want it. Chantelle's a nice girl."

"Okay, if you say so. But if she really doesn't want it, seriously, she'd be the first."

Gideon changes the subject, "Hey, speaking of that, I've been thinking about what you said about your dad. Maybe we should lay low. You know, quit messing around with your servants at least until we know the coast is clear. I'm sort of attached to my balls."

Kai nods. "You're probably right." He stares out the window. His mind flashes to Chantelle practicing for cheer tryouts during last period. She was bent over in all sorts of tantalizing positions. He turns to Gideon. "Maybe we do it one last time?"

"I suggest we quit today, but considering you're pathetic…how sure are you that your dad's not coming home tonight?"

"He said this morning that he'd be back tomorrow night. I think we're pretty safe."

Keiichi lets the boys out at the top of the driveway. They make their way to the front door. Gideon stares in infatuation at the blue fish as Kai unlocks the door.

"Hello, gentlemen."

Kai smiles. "Hi, Oishii."

"Hey," says Gideon.

Koko is in her arms, wrapped up in a towel like a burrito. They see his snout, but his eyes are undetectable.

"Is there anything in particular you and Mr. Gideon would like for afternoon snack, sir?"

Gideon leans over and whispers, "A wet, juicy peach."

Kai knuckles him in the ribs. "Peanut butter and jelly."

Oishii nods politely, then turns away.

"Oh, Oishii?"

"Yes, sir?"

"When will my father be home?"

"Tomorrow night."

They watch her bow swish from side to side as she sashays down the hallway in her six-inch stilettos.

"Lucky pooch," says Gideon.

Kai nudges him. "You should spend the night."

"Really?"

"I've never had anyone sleep over. If you spend the night you can stock up on all the sex you want. Speaking of which, let's go get some."

Gideon asks jokingly, "Before sandwiches?"

He follows Kai into the living room. The colors of the sunset reflect off the pond outside. Gideon wonders if he still has the article on fiber optic light. If so, he may be able to figure out how to install colored light along the creek that runs inside the house.

Kai pushes an intercom.

"Yes, Mr. Tanaka?"

"Oishii, will you and Houseki come to the living room, please?"

The girls giggle, then reply in unison. "Yes, sir."

Kai turns to see Gideon sitting on the couch with his cock already out.

"Which one do you want, dude?"

"I don't care, pussy is pussy, you choose."

"I think you really feel that way, don't you? You're just like my father. They're only objects to you."

"Yep."

The girls appear in the doorway. Kai says something to Oishii in Japanese.

"I want to know what you're telling them."

Houseki walks over to Gideon and gets on her knees.

"I don't need to tell you. You can see what they're doing."

Gideon flops his head back as she takes him into her mouth. He says jokingly, "Come on, dude, speak English. You know I love to hear you talk dirty."

Hours later, Gideon finishes his last bite of halibut. "Man, these girls sure know how to cook." He tosses his napkin over his plate. "Hey, remember, you said earlier today that I could climb that tree in your back yard?"

"No. I said you could have all the sex you want."

"Yeah, that too, after I've climbed the tree."

Kai takes a sip of water. He sets down his glass, and says, "Okay, yeah, let's do it."

"What do you mean, 'let's?' You're Mr. Chicken. Are you telling me you're going to climb that tree?"

"Yep."

"Seriously?"

"Seriously."

"Okay, let's go." Gideon jumps from his chair. He isn't going to wait for Kai to chicken out and change his mind.

They walk through a sliding glass door and head out to the courtyard. The sound of crickets and the bamboo fountain trickling into the pond is peaceful. It's just as serene outside as it was inside. Koko sees the boys and limps over to them, tail wagging.

"Would you mind if I made something for him to help with that limp?"

"I don't mind. Just don't kill him. My father is sort of becoming attached to him."

Craning his neck upward, Kai asks, "How far up do you figure that little platform is?"

Gideon looks up at the tiny white lights illuminating the tree.

"I don't know, ninety, maybe a hundred feet. You can go first, I mean, it is your tree."

"Nah, you're a guest, you go first."

"Okay, but follow right behind me and whatever you do, don't look down."

"Uh, on second thought, maybe I should go first."

"Okay, that way if you faint, I'll catch you."

"Shit! Why'd you have to say that?!"

Gideon laughs. "I'm joking. You'll be fine. Seriously, you'll be fine."

Kai begins the climb. On the tenth rung he looks down at Gideon.

"Dude, what did I just tell you, like, thirty seconds ago?"

"Oh yeah, right, don't look down."

Gideon stays close behind. At the top, Kai crawls onto the platform. He seats himself and clings to the railing.

"It's really cool from up here. I never realized how big our yard is."

"The guard gate looks dinky from here," Gideon says. "I was wondering, is it because of the girls that you have so much security?"

Kai shrugs. "I guess so...to tell you the truth, I'm not really sure."

"I bet you guys have at least thirty or forty acres in your backyard. It doesn't look as big from the front driveway."

They watch Houseki come out to collect Koko. They hear him whine when she picks him up. She consoles him, scratching his head, then heads back into the kitchen to feed him.

"Is he always in pain?"

"I'm not sure. Houseki gives him vitamins, and some kind of Japanese herbs, but it doesn't seem to help much."

Gideon wonders if Japanese herbs would help his headaches.

"I always wanted a dog. Shelly wouldn't even consider it."

Something catches Gideon's eye under the trees. A small building, painted in patches. He can barely see it. It's camouflaged.

"What's that?"

"What?"

"That." He points.

"I don't see anything. You're seeing things."

"No. Over there. Under the trees. See those hedges? There's a building between them. You can just barely make it out."

"Uh, I don't…hey, there's a building over there!"

"Like I said, Mr. you're seeing things."

"How did I never see that before?"

"Why do you suppose it's camouflaged?"

They look at each other, grin, then say in unison, "To keep people out!"

"We should go check it out," Kai says.

"Wait, are YOU actually suggesting we snoop? You wouldn't be getting brave on me, would you?"

"Don't be a faggot."

"You know, it's funny you keep saying that, considering you're the one who isn't making moves on your own girlfriend."

"Dude, that's cold. At least I have a girlfriend."

"I could have one if I wanted. I just don't want one."

Kai snickers. "That's because you're too preoccupied with axing your stepmom, instead of landing some."

"I'd have no problem landing any. I could have plenty of girls."

"Oh yeah, like who?"

"Like Roxanne. Man, she flashes her panties at me every chance she gets. And Christal, every time I go to my locker, she's right there under me. She always gets on her knees to open her locker just so she can stick her face in my crotch. It's like she's begging me to shove my dick in her mouth and unload right down her sweater."

"Yeah, right," Kai says sarcastically.

"What do you mean, right?"

"I mean, how come you haven't asked any of them out?"

Gideon shrugs. "The girls at school are all a bunch of stuck up bitches. They're all trouble if you ask me."

"Trouble?"

"Yeah, I mean most of them are prick teasers. They like getting guys worked up, but when it comes time to put up or shut up, they won't do either."

It occurs to Kai, it's probably best Gideon doesn't have a girlfriend. Girls are complicated. The more he hears Gideon talk about them, the more he wonders if he has the patience for them.

"Hey, Gid, you'd never hurt my father's pets, would you?"

Surprised, Gideon turns toward him. "Are you kidding? Honestly, your dad's pets are the kindest girls I've ever known. I'd never want to hurt them. Having sex with them is my favorite pastime."

Kai announces jokingly, "And so you shall! But first let's go check out the camo' building."

"I swear, dude, you're getting brave on me."

Gideon starts to climb down the rungs. He guides Kai's feet as he descends, reminding him not to look down.

They run around the back of the mansion, then out onto the property. It's pitch black. Gideon can barely make out the hedges. They're nearly invisible.

Kai grabs hold of the tail of Gideon's shirt. "I can't see shit." He hangs onto it as he follows Gideon in the dark.

They walk along the hedge, peering into the darkness until they come to an opening. They slip through it. There's a walkway extending along the edge of the building. Candlelight flickers from a strip of windows high up near the roof line. They tiptoe all around the building looking for a door. There isn't one.

Kai mumbles, "We'd better head back."

"Good idea." It occurs to Gideon that the guards at the gate are armed. If they're mistaken for trespassers, it could get them shot.

Disappointed their quest didn't quite pan out, they return to the mansion and head to Kai's room.

"What do you think is in there?" asks Kai.

"I don't know. The flickering light would suggest someone lives there."

"That's what I was thinking. Hey, maybe Oishii can tell us something."

Kai pushes the intercom button on his wall. Oishii's voice comes over the speaker. "Hello."

"Oishii, would you please come to my room?"

"Yes, sir."

Gideon grins. "After we ask her, can we have some fun with her?"

"Sure."

Seconds later, Oishii is standing at the door.

"Oishii. If I asked you to keep a secret from my father, would you?"

"It depends, sir."

"On what?"

"On your safety. If your life was in danger, I would have to tell."

"But if I wasn't in any danger?"

"It still depends, sir."

66

"Still?" asks Gideon.

"My first loyalty is to my Master. Master Tanaka senior. If you ask me to keep a secret I can do so, but if he specifically asks me, I will have to answer him truthfully. Also, if you ask me to lie to him, and he asks me if you asked me to lie to him, I would have to answer him truthfully."

Kai looks at Gideon. "How likely would it be that my father would ask her a question and then ask her if we told her to lie about that question?"

"Dude, how am I supposed to know? Your dad's a freak."

"Oh yeah, right."

Kai turns to Oishii. "What's in the building on the right side of the mansion? The one that's hidden in the trees?"

"U-" she hesitates. "If Master Tanaka knew I told you, he would beat me senseless."

"You have our word, Oishii, we will never tell him, isn't that right, Gideon?"

"Right, you have my word, too." Gideon recalls the memory of his dad having told him, "A man's word is his bond." Even though he still lies at times, he tells himself white lies don't count.

Oishii studies both of their faces, then says, "Umami Obiat."

"What is that?" Kai asks.

"Not what, master. Who. Very rare possessions of Master Tanaka's. They are the rarest of Obiat, servants.

They've been surgically altered and are stored in that house."

Curious, Gideon asks, "What do you mean stored?"

"They're not like Houseki or me. We're fortunate to be allowed to move about. Umami Obiats do not have as much freedom."

"Can we see them?" asks Kai.

"No, sir. Don't go near them. Your father has hidden cameras all around. Unlike our regular security tapes, he actually checks the Obiat system."

Gideon lowers his head. "Oh, shit, we're done for."

"When father sees us at that building, oh man, I can't imagine what he'll do. I might as well start packing my bags tomorrow." Kai turns to Gideon. "Can I live at your house?"

"Sure. Shelly wouldn't notice. She's too drunk to notice anything."

"Mr. Tanaka? Not to worry, sir. I can change the surveillance tape for the Umami cameras. The guards don't have access to it. They don't even know about it."

"You can do that?" Kai asks.

"Yes."

"Can you erase the security tapes around the mansion?" asks Gideon.

Oishii shakes her head. "No, I'm afraid not. That's a separate system. The security guards give the master a box of tapes once a year. He mentioned just last week that he has two years of tapes to review."

"Crap, what are we going to do? When he finds out you've been here, he'll freak." Kai puts his head between his hands.

Oishii sets her hand on Kai's shoulder. "May I suggest an idea?"

"Yeah. I'll take any idea I can get."

"Me too," says Gideon. His eyes wander over Oishii's sheer pink nightie and matching pink stilettos. *Didn't they buy her any slippers?*

"I've been thinking about what to say if your father finds out Gideon has been here."

"Uh huh…"

"Your father has been helping you with science homework, right?"

Kai nods.

"Tell him because of his help, you've improved your grades so much that your teacher asked you to help another student. Tell him the two of you are study buddies."

Gideon chimes in. "Right, then you can say, remember, dad, I told you I'm helping my study buddy, Gideon. He's amazing!"

Oishii giggles.

Kai smirks at Gideon. "Only an object, huh?"

He turns back to Oishii. "That's a wonderful idea. Father's such an egomaniac that he'll think it's all his doing. Even if he is mad at me for having Gideon over, it would have been for a good reason." Kai glances at Gideon and says jokingly, "He'd probably only cut off one nut for that."

Oishii laughs.

"Man, it's hot in here. Can we go back into the living room?" asks Gideon.

When they get there, Kai says something to Oishii in Japanese.

"Aw man, again with the Japanese! I want to hear what you're telling her."

"You can see what she's doing."

Oishii bends over the couch with her legs spread.

Within seconds, Gideon and Kai have their cocks out. Kai kicks off his shoes and gets up on his knees on the couch in front of Oishii. She takes him in her mouth and begins sucking and licking wildly.

Gideon stands behind her. He runs his hands over her soft white buttocks. Reaching under her, he lets his fingers brush up her inner thighs. The back of his hand slides up against her sex. She arches her back and spreads her legs wider, inviting him to play with her. He begins fondling her. Within a minute, she's wet. He slaps her firmly across the buttocks, leaving a red handprint on her backside.

Kai gets off the couch. "I'll go first."

"Hold on a sec," says Gideon.

He reaches for his slacks to retrieve a packet from his pocket.

"Here, put this on." He hands Kai a condom.

"Why? We haven't needed them before."

"Aren't you curious what it feels like?"

Kai shrugs. "I guess. Where did you get it?"

"Shelly has a case of them in her bathroom."

As Kai fumbles with getting it on, he says, "It doesn't feel as good with a condom."

"I know."

"How do you know?"

"I've tried it."

"You've fucked a girl with one of these?"

"No, I've experimented with a rubber at home."

"You mean, you've jerked off."

"Whatever, dude."

Kai sits down on the couch and leans back. "Get on top, Oishii."

"Play with yourself while he's fucking you," says Gideon.

Holding Oishii's hips, Kai begins moving rhythmically.

Oishii watches Gideon's handsome face as she masturbates.

Gideon grins salaciously. It's like watching a porno with Oishii as the lead. He notices the more excited she becomes, the more aggressive she is with herself. In no time, she begins climaxing.

Kai thrusts faster, and within a minute it's over. He reaches down to hold the edges of the condom as Oishii disengages.

"Get back up on the couch, Oishii. I want to fuck you doggy-style," says Gideon.

On the couch on all fours, Oishii looks over her shoulder and smiles at him.

Gideon grabs her neck, and gently pushes her head down on the couch. Her slit is red and swollen.

"Fuck me, Gideon. Fuck me hard."

Gideon jams his engorged cock into her, stuffing her. He holds her slender hips tight then begins pounding hard and fast.

"Oh! Gideon!" Her insides tighten around him, throbbing up and down his shaft. In no time, Gideon finds himself going over the edge. A wave of pleasure rips through his core. He thrusts violently, emptying himself with each plunge until there's nothing left.

Kai chuckles. "Dude, I think I should always go first. These girls wouldn't feel me otherwise."

"Whatever, man, it's your house. If I have to take sloppy seconds to get some, I'm good with it."

Oishii stands. She crosses her legs tightly as she and Kai converse momentarily in Japanese.

Kai says in English, "Okay, I understand. Thanks, Oishii."

"Yeah, thanks." says Gideon.

She leaves the room.

Gideon nudges Kai. "Hey, we should go check out those Umami girls before Oishii erases the tapes."

"No can do."

"Why not?"

"They'll tell my father."

"How do you know?"

"That's what Oishii was just telling me. She said they can't be trusted. They'll tell. The only way we can see them is if he takes us to them."

Gideon sighs. "Then we'll just have to work on him."

GIDEON MEETS SATORO

Kai answers the phone. "Hello?"

Gideon disguises his voice. "Hello, this is county, STD control."

Kai chuckles. "Hey, Gideon, what's up?"

"Nothin', just bored. I can't go downstairs because the whore is entertaining. Oh wait, I think I just heard the front door slam. Hold on."

Gideon looks out his window and sees a shitty old hatchback pulling out of their driveway.

He picks up the receiver. "The guy just left."

"Uh, can you hold on one sec?" asks Kai.

Gideon hears mumbling on the other end as if Kai is covering the phone with his hand.

"Gideon!"

Aw shit! Shelly's calling me. Not wanting to hang up on Kai, Gideon ignores her.

Kai comes back on the line. "Hey, any chance you'd be available for dinner tonight?"

Jokingly, Gideon says, "Hm, I might be able to pencil you in."

"My father just asked me to invite you."

"Wait, what? Just now?!"

"Uh huh."

Worried, Gideon asks, "Do you think he suspects anything?"

"Nah, he sounded cool."

"You said he's never cool."

Gideon's right. "No, seriously, dude, he was. Besides, if he gets used to you, he might get used to Chantelle. Right now, he refuses to even talk about her."

"Aw, he doesn't want his widdle baby growing up, ha ha!"

"Now you're just being a fucktard," Kai says, annoyed.

"Aw, shit, dude, I got to go. The whore is calling me. Probably wants me help her wax her butt hairs or something."

Kai tries not to visualize it. "You know it's okay not to share, right?"

"So, what time is dinner?"

"Seven."

"Okay, I'll be there."

At six fifty-nine, Gideon rings the Tanaka doorbell. When Oishii answers it, his mouth falls open. She's wearing a drab uniform that covers everything from the knees up. Gideon's eyes drop to her shoes. She's ditched her black stilettos for a pair of black, low-heeled, slip-on shoes. If she had a habit on her head, he'd swear she was a nun.

"Hello, may I help you?" She tilts her head to the side to let Gideon know they're in earshot of Mr. Tanaka.

"Uh, hello. I'm Gideon. I'm here to see Kai and Mr. Tanaka."

"Please come in, Mr. Gideon. They are expecting you."

As Gideon enters, Kai approaches him. Over his shoulder, Gideon sees a very tall man, taller than himself, with wavy, slicked back hair. He's wearing an expensive looking suit and tie. Gideon's glad he had enough sense to wear his dad's old sports coat and button-down shirt.

Lowering his voice he asks Kai, "Is everything cool?"

Kai nods.

As they enter the living room, Kai introduces Gideon. "Father, this is my best friend, Gideon."

Gideon puts his hand out to shake. He makes sure to look Mr. Tanaka in the eye as he greets him, then shakes his hand firmly.

"Hello, Mr. Tanaka. It's nice to meet you."

Mr. Tanaka stares at Gideon's eyes. For an instant, he's drawn to the hints of golden honey which burst into a blue green iris. His eyes are as breathtaking as the shores of the Seychelles. *He's even more attractive than on video.*

"Thank you for coming on such short notice, Gideon."

Kai's dad doesn't look anything like the douchebag Gideon expected. He's much younger looking. The only thing giving away his age is the faint salt and pepper at the temples of his jet black hair.

Mr. Tanaka's odd grin and intense gaze make Gideon imagine what a black panther looks like when a rabbit wanders into its lair. He seems to be looking past the fur and peering right down to the meat.

Mr. Tanaka motions to the couch and chairs. "Why don't we all take a seat and get to know each other?"

As Gideon seats himself on the couch, it occurs to him that the last time he'd sat in this exact spot, Houseki was riding his cock. Images of her straddling him fill his mind. Sitting across from Kai's dad thinking about it feels incredibly awkward. Even more weird is the cat-like grin Mr. Tanaka still has on his face.

Gideon looks at Kai, who's nervously watching his dad. He always assumed Kai exaggerated when he spoke of him, but Mr. Tanaka is just as he'd said, creepy. Like discovering a bit too late the clown holding your hand in the funhouse is squeezing far too hard.

"So, Kai tells me you two are science study buddies."

Sex is a form of biology, so technically that qualifies. "Yes, sir, that's correct." He smiles devilishly at Kai, adding, "Since I've met Kai, I've improved tons."

There's a strange moment of uncomfortable silence.

Nervous, Gideon says, "The fish and the creek you have here are amazing. It's probably a good thing you don't own a cat."

Mr. Tanaka glances at Kai. "Your friend has an interesting sense of humor."

Kai swallows nervously. "Gideon? A sense of humor? Father, he hasn't been able to come up with a good joke in over two years."

Mr. Tanaka's tone changes. He says sharply, "You've been friends for over two years?! Why have you waited all this time to tell me about him?"

Kai cowers. "Sorry, Father, you have a rule."

Chuckling, Mr. Tanaka says, "I'm just messing with you, dude."

Kai and Gideon quicky glance at each other, bewildered, then look to Mr. Tanaka.

"Father, did you just call me dude?"

"Indeed, I did. Isn't that what the two of you call each other?"

"Yes, but you're not my friend. I mean, it's not that you're not my friend, but you're my father, Father."

Gideon's mind races. *How does Mr. Tanaka know what we call each other?*

"I always thought there should be a fine balance of parenting and friendship."

Mr. Tanaka looks to Gideon. "Wouldn't you agree?"

"Uh...uh huh." Gideon shifts uncomfortably, still wondering about Mr. Tanaka's 'dude' remark.

Mr. Tanaka gazes at Kai. "When I was growing up, I hated my father, but I never told him."

Concerned, Kai asks, "You did? Why?"

"Being the smartest, I was his favorite. He started taking me to work when I was ten. I never had time for friends. He even made me work with him on the weekends. As I got older, my life got harder and eventually any friends I had moved on."

"That's so sad, Father."

Mr. Tanaka takes a deep breath, then exhales slowly. "It occurred to me two months ago that I've turned out to be just like him."

"You've never made me work."

"No, but I've been strict. I haven't let you have any friends over."

"You never talk about your family. When you were working, where were your brothers? Didn't they have to work?" asks Kai.

"They were sent to boarding school. Every break they'd come back with stories of beatings by teachers. Back then, that kind of thing was tolerated. If parents complained, their child would be banished from the school. My father was a very strict man. If my brothers complained about school, he would beat them just for verbalizing it."

"That's horrible. You'd never let that happen to me."

"That's right, son. But I haven't been here for you, either."

"It's okay." Kai smiles. "I've got Gideon. He's watched out for me since the day we met."

Mr. Tanaka grins. *Protecting Kai is important to Gideon. I can use that.*

Gideon throws Kai a quick glance. "You'd have done the same for me."

"If it weren't for you, those jerks would still be bullying me."

Mr. Tanaka turns his attention back to his son. "Curious as to what you did with your time, I installed a few surveillance cameras. I'd put them out of my mind until you brought up your study buddy."

Both boys glance in Oishii's direction. She slowly sinks into the drapes behind her.

"Before I continue, is there anything you boys want to tell me?"

Kai looks as if he's seen a ghost. He shakes his head 'no,' then looks down at his feet.

Mr. Tanaka turns to Gideon. He finds his eyes to be incredibly distracting. He watches Gideon's pupils expand and contract as his thoughts scramble.

"Well, actually, sir, we may have broken some rules."

Kai rolls his eyes. *May have? Seriously?*

Appreciating Gideon's honesty, Mr. Tanaka says, "Incidentally, despite what's on the tapes, I want to thank you, Gideon, for keeping Kai out of trouble all this time. I realize now, it's because of you that he's no longer the overly timid boy he once was."

Mr. Tanaka picks up the remote control and turns on the TV.

Gideon looks mortified. The first image is of him fucking Houseki doggy style on the couch. Glancing at the coffee table, he picks up the koi statue. It's been hollowed out from the bottom. He sees the electronics inside. One of the eyes of the fish is slightly glossy. He glances up at Mr. Tanaka, who's watching him.

"The fish have eyes."

Gideon nods and sets it back down.

Turning his attention to the screen, Mr. Tanaka slowly clicks to different images. The next sixty seconds drag like melting ice.

Kai's dad has cameras everywhere. He clicks through various images of their most intimate moments spent with his servants.

Gideon feels the heat rise in his neck. His face is flushed. He glances over at Kai who looks as though he's about to puke.

Mr. Tanaka turns off the TV.

After a long moment of silence, both boys in unison say, "This is my fault."

Gideon turns to Kai. "I mentioned it first. I suggested we fool around with them, remember?"

"No, I mentioned it first. The night we talked about climbing the tree."

"No, dude, it was my birthday party at the pool."

"I'm sure I suggested it first," insists Kai.

"You can't take the blame for this. It was me."

Kai frowns. "You wouldn't have done it if I hadn't brought you over here in the first place."

Impatient, Mr. Tanaka looks to both boys, then interrupts. "Enough."

Houseki is stands in the doorway. "Master?"

"What is it?"

"Dinner is ready."

Mr. Tanaka nods. "We'll be there in a minute." He turns to Gideon. "A family makes up a unit of trust, truthfulness, mistakes, and forgiveness, but most of all, loyalty. Oishii and Houseki may not be our flesh and blood, but Kai and I would protect them at any cost. Because you haven't betrayed our secrets, you're welcome here. I don't want you boys to feel as though you have to sneak around behind my back."

Stunned, Gideon says, "Thank you." He expected to get thrown out of the house.

"Let's continue this discussion over dinner, shall we?"

The boys look dazed.

Gideon can hardly believe it. *After all that, I'm still invited to dinner?*

As Mr. Tanaka stands, the boys rise to their feet. They watch him turn and walk out of the room.

Gideon breathes a sigh of relief. Maybe they wouldn't die after all, at least not until after dinner.

Kai whispers to Gideon, "Dude, I can't believe he didn't chop our heads off! He didn't yell at us or anything. I don't get it."

"Kai!"

The boys immediately scurry to the dining room.

Three settings are closely set in the formal dining room. Mr. Tanaka takes a seat at the head of the table. Each boy takes a seat on either side of him. Gideon glances at the knife next to Mr. Tanaka's plate. He moves his chair just slightly out of reach in case Mr. Tanaka has an urge to go for his jugular.

"I'm disappointed neither one of you had the courage to come forward on your own."

Gideon drops his head. "I'm sorry for what I did." He didn't actually feel sorry for his actions so much as he hated getting caught. It's humiliating.

"I appreciate your apology, Gideon. Mind you, it won't be without consequences." *I'll enjoy taking my time...* "I had a hunch something was going on long before I saw the surveillance tapes."

Gideon wonders, *consequences, what does he mean?*

Kai asks, "Hunch? What kind of hunch?"

"Oishii and Houseki were acting...different."

Mr. Tanaka picks up his knife, gesturing with it. "They got into interesting positions that weren't part of our normal routine. Positions which, as far as I could tell, aren't in any book."

Noticing Gideon's eyes tracking the knife in his hand, Mr. Tanaka turns his attention to him. "Where did you learn such things?"

"I don't know. My brain isn't always in charge."

Mr. Tanaka chuckles, then sets the knife down.

"Tell me what you do in your spare time, Gideon. You know, besides molesting my pets."

Kai interrupts. "His stepmother is an alcoholic and makes him stay up in his room while she visits with all her boyfriends."

"Please allow Gideon to answer, Kai."

Mr. Tanaka turns his attention on Gideon. "Is your stepmother a hooker?"

Sarcastically Gideon replies, "Yeah, the non-profit kind."

The comment makes Mr. Tanaka grin.

Elaborating, Gideon adds, "Her bedroom door is always open if you can stand the stench of fish. They come for the fish and leave with the crabs."

Mr. Tanaka laughs. "Where's your father when all this is going on? Is he away on business?"

"He's dead," says Kai. "His father died seven years ago."

Mr. Tanaka's smile disappears. "I'm sorry, Gideon. What about your mother? Where is she?"

"She died too, Father. In a car accident when he was three."

Mr. Tanaka glares at Kai. He yells something sharply to him in Japanese.

"It's okay, Kai, I can answer for myself. It's not so bad anymore, you know, talking about them. I miss them, though."

Mr. Tanaka softens his tone. "I'm very sorry for your loss, Gideon." *This couldn't be more perfect.* "Do you have any other blood relatives? Any aunts or uncles around?"

"No, sir."

Excellent.

"Father, he's going to kill his stepmom."

Annoyed, Gideon barks, "Kaa-ii!"

"Father wouldn't tell anyone. Besides, dude, you know about his pets. Why would he tell on you?"

Mr. Tanaka's tone is menacing. "You're not helping your situation, son."

Kai recoils.

Mr. Tanaka peers at Gideon with great interest. He leans toward him on one forearm. "So, tell me, why do you want to kill her?"

"When Shelly married my dad, he was healthy, then all of a sudden he got very sick. He was put on bed rest." Bitterly, Gideon's adds, "After he died, she told people she only married him because he was rich."

Curious, Mr. Tanaka asks, "What was the official cause of his death?"

"Poison." Gideon stares down at his placemat. "The police questioned her but didn't have enough evidence to charge her."

Raising an eyebrow, Mr. Tanaka sits back in his chair. This is becoming far more interesting than just the forbidden liberties going on under his roof.

"So, now you want revenge."

Gideon nods.

"Tell me, how do you plan to kill her?"

Wanting to get off the subject, Gideon shrugs. "I'm not sure yet. I'm still working it out."

"He has a list, Father. He carries it with him everywhere." Kai waves his hand, motioning to Gideon, "Go on, show him."

Annoyed, Gideon frowns at him. *Dude, seriously, what the fuck?*

"This list," asks Mr. Tanaka. "May I see it?"

Gideon reluctantly retrieves his wallet from his pocket. He pulls out his '100 ways' list and hands it over.

Mr. Tanaka studies it thoughtfully. "Hm, very impressive. It appears you have many talents indeed. I'm fascinated." Glancing up at Gideon, he adds, "I like this note you have here." He points to a footnote at the bottom. "Very insightful." *His imagination has no limits.*

"I don't have all the details yet. I could just wait for her to pass out, but she'd just die."

Smiling, Mr. Tanaka asks, "Isn't that the point?"

"What I mean is, she wouldn't suffer the way my dad suffered."

"That's all he does, Father." Kai rolls his eyes. "He spends all his time thinking about how he's going to whack his stepmother."

Mr. Tanaka's eyes dart to Kai. "That's not all he does, or you for that matter."

Like a guilty dog, Kai looks away from him.

"You know, Gideon, it was my first inclination to banish you from Kai's life when I saw you on those videos. But after contemplating it, your contribution to his life far outweighs any rules that may have been broken here."

"I'm lucky to have his friendship." Gideon looks over at Oishii and Houseki, then back to Mr. Tanaka. "All of yours, actually. If it weren't for this family, I wouldn't have anyone."

And we have you… "I may be able to help you with that last item on your list."

86

"Father, you're not seriously--"

Mr. Tanaka puts his hand up to silence Kai. "This doesn't concern you. This is between Gideon and me."

Gideon notices the cat-like grin again as Mr. Tanaka says, "A friend of Kai's is a friend of mine."

Oishii sets a glass of water next to Mr. Tanaka's wine. He glances up at her and says menacingly, "I'll deal with you and Houseki later."

As she turns to head back to the kitchen, Gideon can tell she's upset. *She's in deep shit.*

Oishii passes Houseki, who's holding plates of food. She whispers in her ear. Gideon can tell she too is upset. She sets the plates down and returns to the kitchen.

Motioning toward the food, Mr. Tanaka says, "Please eat, while it's still hot."

The boys pick at their dinner.

"Come on, I'm not going to kill you. Eat!"

"Mr. Tanaka? Will Oishii and Houseki be punished for, you know, playing around with us?"

"Yes. Severely, I'm afraid."

Gideon looks down at his plate, contemplating what he can do to keep the girls from hating him.

"I'd like to take their punishments." He glances up at Mr. Tanaka. "That is, if it's okay with you."

Kai looks at Gideon, astonished.

Surprised by Gideon's comment, Mr. Tanaka wonders, *Why would he offer to take the punishment of a servant?*

87

He's never heard of such a thing. Leaning forward, he asks, "Why would you want to do that?"

"It isn't their fault."

"I thought you said it's all just pussy to you!" snaps Kai.

"It is, dude, but since they're servants, were they going to say no? I'll take their punishments."

Gideon looks at Mr. Tanaka. "That is, if you permit it."

"Fine," says Kai, annoyed. He turns to his father. "Me too, Father."

Impressed by Kai's loyalty, Mr. Tanaka says, "You understand I won't go easy on you boys just because you volunteered to do this?" Mr. Tanaka rubs his chin thoughtfully. "All right. You must agree right now to accept any punishment, no matter what it is, without backing out for any reason. You'll do exactly as you're told." *Especially you, Gideon.* "If you can accept those terms, I'll allow it."

Gideon doesn't hesitate. "I accept."

Butterflies of excitement stir in Mr. Tanaka's belly.

There's silence from Kai's side of the table.

Mr. Tanaka turns to his son. "Kai, do you still want to take a punishment?"

"Uh…"

His father's voice is harsh. "Yes or no?!"

Kai looks down at his plate. "Yes, Father."

Mr. Tanaka sits back in his seat. "Very well. This is unusual. I'm very busy these days. It will take a little time to come up with a meaningful punishment."

Gideon's relieved the girls are spared.

Kai takes another bite of his dinner but the food seems to have lost its taste. He wonders if connecting his father with his psycho best friend wasn't the best idea.

When the boys are done with their dinner, Mr. Tanaka says, "Let's have coffee in my office, shall we?"

He nods to Oishii. She goes into the kitchen to prepare it.

Surprised, Kai asks, "You're actually going to let us in your office? You've never let me go in there."

"You're a man now, Kai. I didn't let you go in there when you were little because there are passages where you could get lost or hurt. I also didn't want the girls to get hurt looking for you."

"I didn't ever think of that."

Mr. Tanaka looks to both boys. "I hope I'm making myself clear when I say neither of you are to take advantage of Oishii or Houseki without my permission, understood?"

The boys respond solemnly, "Yes, sir."

"Can I be excused, Father? I told Chantelle I'd call her at eight thirty."

Mr. Tanaka takes a deep breath. It's all very disturbing to him. Kai having people in his life and his not being aware of it until recently.

"Of course." He frowns as he watches Kai leave.

Gideon notices Mr. Tanaka's tic. This is the third time he caught him tilting his head awkwardly sideways and back again.

Oishii returns to fill her master's wine glass.

She sets a plate with a chocolate cookie in front of Gideon.

"Thank you." He picks it up and takes a small bite.

Gideon pretends not to notice Mr. Tanaka watching him intently. He looks around, wondering why there's a strip of grass growing in the formal dining room. He scans the art work on the wall, attempting to decipher the artist's thoughts, as he slowly nibbles around the edge of his cookie in small, even bites.

Mr. Tanaka wonders how difficult it will be to influence him. Picking up his wine glass, he thinks to himself, *How ironic. What I've searched years to find has been sneaking in and out of my own home.*

"Thank you for dinner," Gideon says. "It was delicious."

Oishii and Houseki enter the dining room and begin clearing plates.

"You're welcome. The coffee should be done any minute. Wait here, Gideon. I have something for you. I'll be right back."

With Mr. Tanaka out of the room, Gideon whispers to Houseki, "What should I talk about?"

Knowing her master, he'll try to manipulate Gideon.

"Just be yourself."

Oishii chimes in, "Let him win. He needs to feel that he's in control of the situation."

"That's good advice," agrees Houseki. "Let him control the conversation, and just be yourself."

Mr. Tanaka returns with a small book.

"I'd like you to have this. When a friend died, it was given to me to help me through the loss."

"Thank you." Gideon places it inside his sport coat pocket.

Sensing his reluctance to look at it, Mr. Tanaka says, "It's clear you're a bright young man. Whatever you've accomplished in life, no one can take it from you. But don't delude yourself into thinking you don't need anyone in life, or refrain from asking for help when you need it. I'd not be as successful as I am had it not been for the people who've helped me along the way."

Gideon nods. No one has ever put it like that, or spoken to him that way. Maybe he'll read the book after all.

"Let's head to my office then, shall we?"

OFFICE CHAT

Gideon follows Mr. Tanaka as they descend a rock staircase into a large wine cellar. At the back of the cellar, there's a small archway with an iron gate. As they pass through it, they descend more stairs. At the bottom, there are other gates with tunnels that extend into the darkness. The earthy smell and the chill in the air, tells Gideon they are underground.

They arrive at an ornately carved door. The carving is a huge, black, embossed dragon tail, rising six inches off the face of the door. The tree it was carved from must have been enormous. Gideon glances up. Above the door, carved in black stone, is the back end of the dragon's body. It appears to be crawling into a cave above the door.

"Wow, that is the coolest thing ever."

Mr. Tanaka smiles. "Thank you. I designed it myself."

Entering a code on the key pad, Mr. Tanaka pushes open the door. He motions for Gideon to go ahead.

As Gideon wanders in, he sees the office is a massive stone cave. He surveys the ceiling, then glances left to right from wall to wall. There are no pillars to brace anything, yet up on the ceiling is an massive chandelier. There are no exposed wires. He wonders how they managed to hang it.

Mr. Tanaka observes Gideon's interest in the structure of the room.

"I'm curious to know what you're passionate about, Gideon."

Knowing he's smarter than most adults, Gideon says modestly, "I like dabbling in electronics and chemistry."

"Is that so?"

"Uh huh. My mom used to teach chemistry early in her career. Her lab is in the basement of our house."

"Perhaps you'll follow in her footsteps."

"Yeah, maybe. I spend a lot of time down there on account of my stepmother being too afraid to go in the basement."

"Why won't she go there?"

"Well, for one thing, she doesn't know what a circuit breaker is. I flip it off when I leave the lab. I told her that rats have chewed through the wiring and to be careful not to step on one."

Mr. Tanaka chuckles. "Very clever."

"Once in a while I'll wad the end of a loaf of bread and cover it with hair from her hair brush. I toss it in a baggie to show her the dead rat." Gideon laughs. "She totally freaks."

"Ingenious, I like it."

Frowning, Gideon adds, "My dad has old electronics magazines down there. Shelly would toss them out if she got her hands on them."

It seems to Satoro that Gideon is unusually nostalgic for his age. Protecting the shreds of materials relating to the memories of his parents and their accomplishments are quite important to him.

"What about video games? It seems to be the pastime for young men your age these days."

"Shelly thinks they're a waste of money. I've enjoyed playing them here with Kai though." Gideon looks down at his feet and mumbles, "Of course, you already know that."

Mr. Tanaka places his hand on Gideon's shoulder.

"I'll let you in on a little secret. There's not much that ever goes on without my eventually knowing about it."

The comment makes Gideon smirk. *If he actually knew all the shit I've done, he'd never let me hang out with Kai.*

Mr. Tanaka senses he's hit a button. *Gideon has secrets.*

They walk to the fireplace at the far end of the cave. Gideon glances at the small alcove with a built-in bar and fridge.

"This is the coolest office ever."

"The toilet is on the right, through there if you need to use it." Mr. Tanaka points to a small hallway.

Gideon nods. "Thanks, I'm good." He sets himself down on the purple velvet couch, then leans over to touch the table. Cold and smooth, it's a massive chunk of amethyst. It must have cost a fortune.

Mr. Tanaka takes a seat in the sand colored velvet chair beside him. He notices Gideon rubbing his temples.

"Headache?"

"Yeah, I get them now and then. I'll be fine."

There's a knock on the door.

"Come in!"

Oishii opens the door, carrying a tray between her arm and her hip. "It's so cold in here," she says. Upon setting down the tray, she places a napkin, a small gold spoon, and a cup in front of Gideon. It's topped with fluff.

Mr. Tanaka receives a clean wine glass. Both men watch as Oishii opens a fresh bottle of wine.

"Will there be anything else, Master?"

"A pain reliever for Gideon."

Oishii retrieves a red pill from one of the cabinets. She sets it in front of Gideon with a small glass of water, then wraps herself in a small cashmere blanket and sits in a chair in the corner.

"Do you see spots when the headaches come on?"

Gideon nods. He tosses the pill to the back of his throat, then washes it down with water.

"More like flashes of light."

"Migraines. Anything can trigger them, but eating regularly does tend to help."

Yeah, that's never going to happen. Gideon expects coffee, but when he sips through the fluff, it's the richest hot chocolate he's ever tasted.

"Wow, that's good."

Mr. Tanaka gets up from his seat. He reaches into a cabinet, then returns with a small glass bottle of brown liquid. He pours a few drops into Gideon's drink, then stirs it with the teaspoon. Reaching into his pocket, he retrieves a small vial containing blue liquid. Using a dropper, he adds three drops, then stirs.

"Now try it."

Picking it up, Gideon sniffs it suspiciously.

"Try it!" says Mr. Tanaka harshly.

Gideon takes another sip. It tastes richer somehow. There's a slight burning in his throat. He smiles. "Thank you, it's delicious."

"Are you into sports, Gideon?"

"Not really. I'm not a crowd type of person. I like puzzles and crosswords, and I read a ton."

After a few minutes of chit-chat, Gideon begins to feel warm. He asks Mr. Tanaka if he wouldn't mind if he takes off his sportscoat.

"Sure." *Take it all off.* "The fire tends to warms things up in here pretty fast."

Gideon removes his sportscoat and sips his drink again.

Moments later, Mr. Tanaka also gets up and removes his jacket. He loosens his tie and begins rolling up his sleeves. Gideon notices he has a couple of small tattoos on his arm. Symbols of some kind.

Oishii quickly rushes over to take Mr. Tanaka's sportscoat.

Gideon watches her as she returns to her corner like an obedient dog.

"I often wonder what it would be like to have pets like yours. I think it would be cool having three or four of them."

"I'm curious, Gideon. If you had four girls and they all turned on you at once, what would you do to control them?"

"Oh gee, maybe spike their drinks or something." As he says it, he realizes how relaxed he feels after just a few sips of his chocolate.

"And, what would you do with them after they were sedated?" Mr. Tanaka's eyes wander over him, letting his imagination grow.

"I'd, you know, get all the sex I want, then do number 10, 14, 15, and 18."

"Let me see that list again."

Gideon pulls the list from his wallet and hands it to Mr. Tanaka.

Mr. Tanaka studies it. "You're somewhat of a romantic aren't you?"

"What makes you say that?"

"Your list, it seems rather...personal."

Gideon slurs his words slightly as he says, "Yeah, it is personal. For that kind of thing, I'd make a new list though."

"Why? It seems to me the list you have is sufficient."

"First off, each girl is different. For example, if a girl is a mouthy bitch who talks like my stepmom, I'd slash her throat and hang her upside down so she's a mess when they find her. There's nothing romantic about that."

"Indeed." Mr. Tanaka is delighted by Gideon's imagination. "Custom tailored to the individual." *He thinks on his feet...probably very receptive.*

Mr. Tanaka notices Gideon glancing at his tattoos. He holds his arm out to give him a better look.

"They're good luck symbols. Kai has this same tattoo. He hates it. It's inside his upper arm where it's not noticeable. Don't tell him I told you. He's pretty sensitive about it."

Gideon nods. He's only seen Kai take his shirt off once. Now he knows why.

"Tell me about Shelly."

"She's disgusting. You should see some of the filth that walks into our house."

Gideon notices Mr. Tanaka frowning.

"I'm sorry. You invited me to dinner and all I've been doing is bitching about my stepmom."

"You're not bitching."

Gideon grins as he leans toward Mr. Tanaka. "Want to hear something funny about her, though?"

Mr. Tanaka leans over and picks up Gideon's drink. Handing it to him, he stares at his intoxicating eyes.

"Yes, please tell me."

Gideon takes another sip, then another. He sets his drink down.

"Okay, so one day I came downstairs and I heard her in her bedroom talking. Her door was cracked open an inch or so, so I went to snoop. She was saying, 'Buttons, momma's in heat. Here Buttons, momma's in heat.' So, I think to myself, 'What the fuck?' Oh, sorry, sir, please excuse my cursing."

He picks up his cup. "What's in this drink?"

"A special liquor is all. Continue, please. What's happening with Buttons?"

Gideon takes another sip, then continues. "Well, I thought to myself, w.t.f.?! I look through the crack in her bedroom door and she's holding Buttons."

"Who's Buttons?"

"It's her nasty stuffed animal. It used to sit in the back window of her car. Well, that is, until she totaled it." Gideon shakes his head, giggling as he talks about it. "The drunk bitch wrapped it around a tree. She managed to save Buttons, but she lost her license. Anyway, she's holding Buttons..." Gideon laughs again, trying to control himself as he attempts to finish his sentence. "She's holding that nasty cat between her legs and--" He bursts out laughing again.

Mr. Tanaka laughs along with him.

Gideon catches his breath and continues. "So, she's trying to fuck her fake fur cat. I'm sure that thing has been all over the floor of her dirty car and all over her filthy room. She's talking to it, rocking herself on it and--"

He laughs uncontrollably. His belly hurts and he feels dizzy. He tries to stop laughing but can't control himself. It all seems sadly hilarious to him. With tears in his eyes, he leans over on one elbow, half lying on the couch.

"It's really not even that funny, yet every time I think about it, it's so horrific, it makes me laugh because, well, this is my life and I have to live with her. It's so messed up."

Mr. Tanaka leans toward him. He smiles and asks, "Have you ever hurt anyone, Gideon?"

Through his laughter Gideon says, "Oh yeah, but only because they deserved it."

"Have you ever thought about hurting my servants or telling anyone about them?"

Surprised by the question, Gideon says, "And lose my hot fuck buddies? Aw, hell no!"

Mr. Tanaka motions to Oishii. She brings over a small glass of water and hands it to her master.

He pulls a purple glass bottle from his pocket and places three drops into the water. Holding Gideon's head up, he sets the water to his lips. *Those lips...slightly parted, panting...*

"Drink!" he orders.

Gideon drinks all of it, then lies back down on the couch. He begins speaking incoherently, then breaks out in cheerful giggles.

Kai enters the office. "Sorry I was on the phone so long."

He bends over Gideon, peering at him like a concerned parent. With a raised eyebrow, he asks, "Dude, are you drunk?"

Gideon's watery eyes glance up. "What gave me away?"

"He'll be back on his feet in twenty minutes, when the antidote kicks in."

"What was it?"

"Nothing horrible, just a truth serum."

"Seriously? That's messed up!"

"I had to do it, Kai, for my own peace of mind. I had to make sure he's okay. We have to protect our family."

Kai glances down at Gideon who's passed out in a drunken slumber. "You don't know him like I do! He'd have agreed to take it himself. He'd have understood."

Mr. Tanaka slips a pillow under Gideon's head as he ponders his son's assessment. *He'd have agreed to take it?*

"I hate the thought of him living with that awful woman." Mr. Tanaka glances at Kai, realizing he just blurted out something his son might repeat.

"Don't repeat that, son."

"I won't. He'd appreciate that you care, though."

"I'm serious. Not one word. I can't help if you start blabbing my concerns."

"You'll help him? Oh, thank you, Father."

"I can't promise anything. But I'll look into it."

Gideon barely stirs when Mr. Tanaka and Kai stand him up to get him into the service elevator. They remove his shoes and pants, and lay him on Kai's bed. Kai covers him with his comforter.

"I'll sleep on the daybed in the corner. Good night, Father."

"Good night, son."

The next morning all Gideon remembers is having a drink in the office with Mr. Tanaka.

Sitting at the kitchen table, he asks Oishii, "Was I horrible last night?"

"You were perfect."

"Really? I wasn't obnoxious?"

"Not at all. I want to thank you, Gideon, for agreeing to take punishments for me and Houseki. It's very honorable of you."

"It was the right thing to do."

"Would you like some breakfast?"

"Just some toast, then I need to go. I want to get out of here before Mr. Tanaka wakes up. I can't face him after last night."

"He left this morning. He was in rather good spirits I must say."

"Really? He isn't upset that I was drunk?"

"Of course not. He was the one giving you alcohol."

"How did I get into bed?"

"Master Tanaka and Kai helped you. You were a little wobbly."

"Was I sick?"

"No. Here, drink this. You'll be like new in ten minutes."

"Ugh! It's awful! What is it?"

"Charcoal, vitamins, and wheatgrass. It's a Japanese version of what they call 'hair of the dog'. Good for a hangover."

Mr. Tanaka gazes at the city through his twenty-sixth floor window. Life is a game of chess; it pays to have a strategy. He has been brewing one up all morning. An elaborate plan, which always tends to be expensive but, in the end, well worth it. He picks up the phone.

"Rai, will you step into my office?"

A moment later, he hears the keypad outside his door. Rai walks in carrying his usual pen and pad of paper. He closes the door behind him.

"Good morning, sir."

"Good morning. Beautiful day, isn't it?"

Rai looks up. *This is new.*

"Why yes, sir. It is." He waits, hoping Mr. Tanaka will elaborate on his good mood.

"I'd like you to write in your own shorthand and destroy your notes as things are accomplished."

"Absolutely. How can I be of service?"

"We're going to set up a ruse."

"A ruse? You mean like, 'Tokyo in October'?"

"Yes, only the scenario is very different. Let's use the girl from before. She has the right skills for the task. I'll need her for two to three days."

"I'll see if she's available."

"We'll need a new male. Someone who's weird, disturbing, yet refined."

Rai grins. *You mean like you?*

Mr. Tanaka adds, "Make him a foreigner."

"Any type in particular, sir?"

Taking a moment to think about it, Mr. Tanaka says, "Make him Romanian or something along those lines. A fortyish male, attractive, aristocrat type, but disturbing."

Rai nods as he writes frantically, making sure to get all the details.

Mr. Tanaka watches Rai's pen race across the paper. His writing is artful. Beautiful rolling lines with a mix of occasional dagger-like strokes.

Rai looks up. "What's his directive?"

"For now, just an acquaintance."

"How long do you anticipate using him?"

"Once things begin to roll, only a day or two. Depending on how things progress, maybe longer. He'll need a designer suit and uh…a tuxedo."

Mr. Tanaka chuckles to himself, mumbling, "A tuxedo will be perfect."

"Got it."

"Oh, another thing. Have I.T. set up a website to establish some legitimacy. Make him an investor."

Rai nods, scribbling rapidly. *Bogus legitimacy. Got to love it.*

"And salary?"

"The female will receive fifty thousand for two days."

Rai says under his breath, "Fifty k, just for shutting up."

"The male will receive a payment of a hundred thousand. Make it up front with a bonus upon completion."

Sexist…

Mr. Tanaka waits until Rai finishes writing.

"Maybe I'll buy him an island or something."

Rai looks up, "An island? Really? Can I do it?"

"No, I need you here. Besides, I was just kidding about the island."

Mr. Tanaka, kidding? That too is new.

They hear a *ting* alerting them that the next appointment has arrived.

Rai looks at his watch. "Looks like your eleven o'clock is here."

"Just let me know when you find him. We can work out the rest of the details later. In the meantime, figure out a total budget for travel and supplies, and have Kimmy open an expense account."

"Yes, sir."

Rai gets up to leave.

"You have the shareholder meeting at two o'clock and a conference call with the Navy at five."

As Rai reaches the door, Mr. Tanaka says, "Wait five minutes before sending in my next appointment."

Rai nods, closing the door behind him.

Mr. Tanaka checks his watch. He slips into the back room to change.

When he enters his office again, he's wearing a black silk robe, nothing else. He checks the wall clock. Only five seconds to go. He hears the familiar buzz as Rai sends the man in.

The young executive rushes in. He's dressed in a black suit, white shirt, and blue tie. Without a word, he undresses in front of Mr. Tanaka, then falls to his knees facing him.

Mr. Tanaka pulls a thick strap from his bottom desk drawer.

"You're five minutes late!" He wields the strap over his shoulder and vigorously sends it down across the young man's back.

Driver's Ed

The day has finally come when most teens can barely wait to get behind the wheel, yet Gideon finds himself feeling perturbed.

"Feel the clutch as you let it out."

Along with stalling Mr. Tanaka's car for the hundredth time, the sound of Ms. Pinkberry's voice is increasingly annoying. Gideon cringes as he grinds the gears yet again on the borrowed Mercedes.

"Relax, you're trying to push it," says Ms. Pinkberry. "Try to feel the car's vibration as you release the pedal under your foot."

Gideon looks down at Ms. Pinkberry's tan legs and the beads of sweat on her thighs. Her short dress barely covers her crotch.

He starts the car again, this time feeling the clutch as he slowly lets it out. The car purrs and rolls forward.

Ms. Pinkberry rummages into her purse to retrieve her lipstick. While dragging it across her top lip she says, "Pull out, onto County Road. There's less traffic."

Gideon turns onto the interstate. He takes a deep breath. *As long as I don't have to stop, I'll be fine.*

Ms. Pinkberry begins fumigating the car with her perfume.

Gideon rolls down his window, hoping to let the fresh air in. His mind wanders to a conversation he overheard earlier that day in the guy's locker room.

Larry and two other guys had gone from talking about the hot cheerleaders, to the new horny M.I.L.F. in Driver's Ed. "You should have seen her," said Larry. "The other day, she leans over to get my certificate from the bottom drawer in her file cabinet. You know how short her dresses are, right?"

They all nod.

"She bent over and she wasn't wearing any panties."

They laugh and huddle together to avoid being overheard. Gideon didn't hang out with them. They just happened to be standing right behind his P.E. locker, which is adjacent to Larry's.

"I don't think she was even aware she'd forgotten them because she just kept talking to me."

Yeah right, she forgot her panties. That's about as likely as a fat kid forgetting about the candy bar in his pocket.

By the end of the conversation, all three dopes decided she was just an 'airhead'. It's astounding to Gideon how easily guys are taken in by a nice piece of ass.

She's a vulture who knows exactly what she's doing.

Rumor was, if a student didn't have sex with her, she wouldn't sign the driver's certificate. She'd already been fucked by half the student body.

"You're doing great, Gideon." She puts her hand on his knee, bringing him back to the present.

Despite most guys finding Ms. Pinkberry attractive, Gideon is repulsed by her. Then it hits him, *she's just another Shelly.*

Moments later she digs her nails into his leg, running them up his thigh.

He glances over at her.

"Ms. Pinkberry, what are you doing?"

"Keep your eyes on the road. Just relax."

He flexes his leg in defense against her nails.

"Watch your speed." She attempts to sound sweet, but her tone is artificial.

"That's distracting. Can you please stop it?"

"A good driver needs to be able to deal with unexpected distractions, Gideon."

He tries focusing on something else. There's nothing but road and trees. He sticks his head halfway out the window, searching for the smell of the pine, but her fucking perfume is too stifling. It makes his head hurt.

"Should I turn around and head back?"

"No!" she snaps. "I've got someplace special in mind."

Aw shit.

Turning her body toward him, she unbuttons the top of her dress.

"Can you please stop doing that?"

She laughs, ignoring him.

He reaches down and turns up the air conditioner, hoping she'll cover up.

Her claws move toward his crotch. He can feel himself getting hard. It isn't helping his predicament.

Gideon thinks back to last week when they went over the controls. Ms. Pinkberry kept reaching over, adjusting the lights, the mirrors, playing with switches on the steering wheel, 'accidentally' bumping into his crotch. She'd been practically molesting him for weeks. Today it seems, she intends to get what she wants. If he didn't need her to sign his certificate, he'd report her.

"Turn left, Gideon." He glances over at her and notices her dress is now unbuttoned down to her waist, exposing her lace bra and the cleavage stuffed inside it.

They come to an intersection. *Oh, shit.* As he hits the brakes, he looks to Ms. Pinkberry for instruction as to which way to turn.

She unbuckles her seat belt and pivots her body so that her back is against the passenger door. She rests her foot on the seat, then pulls up her dress.

Does she not own any panties?! Her thighs are wet, she's wet. She puts her fingers between her legs and looks up at him.

"You can do this," she says.

Down shifting, Gideon grinds the gears and stalls again. *Dammit!* He puts it into park and restarts the engine. Thankfully, the car doesn't jerk. He continues driving straight.

"Good boy." She begins fondling herself.

Gideon looks at the clock on the dash. Ten to three. *Obviously, I won't be her first fuck of the day.*

"At least put your seat belt back on, Ms. Pinkberry."

She laughs, ignoring him.

Fuck, she's an asshole. The throbbing in his head is progressively worse.

He rubs his left temple.

"Do you have any aspirin?" he asks.

She ignores him. Too busy masturbating to care.

Panting, she says, "Soon you'll come to a blue tank..." She sits forward. "There. Turn right, right here."

The blue metal tank is barely noticeable. Had she not pointed it out, he'd have missed it.

She settles herself back into the seat, then pulls off her sandals and sets her feet up on the dashboard.

His face reddens. *This isn't my car!* He doesn't want her nasty feet on the dash.

He comes to the end of the paved road where it turns into a wide dirt path. They haven't seen any houses for miles.

He slows down, asking impatiently, "Now where?"

"Just keep driving straight. You'll come to a small field a short way up the road. There's a creek nearby. That's where you'll fuck me."

Gideon rolls the car slowly onto the dirt road.

"I don't want to touch you, let alone screw you."

"You will, if you hope to get your certificate."

Manipulative bitch.

His head feels like it's going to explode. He can't face having to tell Mr. Tanaka he blew it. It was embarrassing enough asking to borrow his car. Besides, what's he going to say? *A milf teacher is sexually harassing me?* No, he has to handle this by himself and hope that getting his certificate doesn't come with an STD.

The field is now in sight. Before turning off, he sees the road continues on quite a ways. *Wonder how much farther it goes?*

Ms. Pinkberry asks, "Do you have a blanket?" She pulls her sandals back on.

Parking the car, Gideon gets out and checks in the trunk. Mr. Tanaka has a red wool blanket neatly folded inside.

He grabs it and walks around to the passenger door.

As Ms. Pinkberry starts to get out, Gideon pushes her back down into the seat. "First sign my certificate, or I won't fuck you."

She smirks, "First fuck me, and then I'll sign it."

Unzipping his pants, he pulls his cock free. "You see this? I can go at it all afternoon. If you want it, sign my certificate and let's get to fucking already."

She stares at the thick veins on his cock, then reaches into her purse and pulls out a blank certificate and her pen.

Signing her name at the bottom, she sets it on the dash. She gives him a flirtatious look and he steps back to let her out.

Tucking his cock inside his slacks, he then grabs her hand. She giggles as he yanks her along, making his way to the far end of the field.

Holding two corners of the blanket, he snaps it in the air and lays it out neatly on the grass. He would have told her to take off her dress, but she's already pulling it over her head.

"Get on your knees. I want to fuck you from behind."

"I like it on top," she says sternly.

Gideon peers at her. "And you'll get it, but first I want to take you from behind."

Amused by Gideon's attempt to take charge, she says, "Fine." She kneels down onto the blanket, then leans forward on her knees. Holding her weight with one hand, she begins masturbating with the other.

Gideon picks up her dress and removes the cloth tie. He looks down at her beautiful suntanned body. *What a waste.* He drops to his knees and jimmies up behind her.

"Mmm," she moans and wiggles her butt over the bulge in his pants.

He wraps each end of the tie around a fist and quickly reaches over her head. By the time she realizes what's happening, he's able to get it twice around her neck. She struggles, but the more she tries to pull away, the tighter the noose becomes. Reaching back, she attempts to pull his hair and scratch him.

He knees her hard in the back, then tucks his head in between her shoulder blades so she can't scratch his eyes or face. He presses his fingers deep down into her carotid arteries.

She grabs at her neck, frantic for air, but can't get her fingers under the tie. She gasps, until she finally passes out.

Gideon holds his position until his fingers just can't apply pressure any longer. When he releases his grip, her body slinks down onto the blanket.

He flips her face up, and checks her pulse. Nothing. Eyes swollen and bloodshot, they stare lifelessly up at the sky. Not taking any chances, he picks up a rock and sends two powerful blows to her throat, breaking her windpipe.

He sits back on his haunches and takes several deep breaths. His anger quickly fades. He feels oddly peaceful, serene. His headache is gone. He sits for a long time trying to make sense of it all. Feeling no remorse, no fear, he decides none of this is his fault. *I'm the victim. All I did was take my power back.*

He walks back to the car and retrieves his backpack. He finds the tissue containing Mr. Smith's pen. Returning to Ms. Pinkberry's body, he pulls Mr. Tanaka's blanket from underneath her. She rolls slightly with her upper torso on its side. Gideon shakes the pen free from the tissue, onto the grass. He places his foot against Ms. Pinkberry's back and gently shoves her face down on top of it.

Gathering the tissue, the rock, and her clothes, he wraps them inside the blanket. Back at the car, he sets the blanket and Ms. Pinkberry's purse into Mr. Tanaka's trunk. He checks the certificate on the dash. It's undated. He decides he'll backdate it by a week.

When he gets to the house, he calls out for Houseki. She comes immediately. She can tell by his face something's wrong.

"What? What's happened?"

"I need your help. Ms. Pinkberry, she's… I swear it isn't my fault."

Houseki stares horrified at the blanket and purse.

"You have to believe me. Please…help me. You're the only one I can trust."

Her mind races to Gideon standing up for her and Oishii. It was a kind thing for him to do, offering to take their punishments. This had to be some kind of accident. Gideon would never intentionally hurt anyone.

"I can burn them," she says.

He nods, handing over the items.

"I have to get back to school."

"You must never speak of this, Gideon. Not to anyone, ever."

"I won't."

He drives back to school and quickly heads to Ms. Pinkberry's office. Using his shirt hem, he opens the bottom drawer of her file cabinet and places his certificate below several others. Scanning the office, he considers what else he should do.

Her white board reads, "Student Lesson - Back in 1 hour." He erases the board.

Remembering that she keeps a desk calendar, he goes over and rips off the top page with all of her student appointments. He tears off the next page as well, ensuring no indentations are left behind.

When he gets home, he rips the pages into tiny pieces over the toilet bowl, then flushes until there is nothing left.

Replaying the afternoon in his head, Gideon mulls over the details. *Was there anything left undone?* Anything at all that could tie him to Ms. Pinkberry.

PUNISHMENT CONTRACT

A few days later Gideon is at his locker to unload his books from his backpack. He sees Kai approaching from the opposite end of the hallway. His face is full of apprehension.

"What's up with you?" Gideon asks.

"Don't freak but…"

"What?"

"My father is calling a meeting tonight…and uh, he invited Shelly."

"What? Why?"

"He said he needs her permission. He's going to have her sign some kind of form."

"Permission? For what?"

"I'm not sure, but he wants you to come."

Gideon laughs, "I wonder if she'll tell him to fuck off or if she'll actually show up."

"He sent our driver to your house to hand deliver the invitation."

As soon as she sees the Bentley, she'll break out her shovel.

Gideon laughs. "She's a gold digging bitch. When she sees Keichii, she'll smell money. Your dad's smart."

"Yeah, and he doesn't take 'no' for an answer. If she said 'no,' he'd probably grab her by the hair and drag her to our house himself."

"Really?"

Exasperated, Kai says, "I've never been able to predict what he'll do."

"Why doesn't the driver just ask her to sign the form?"

"Father invites people over when he wants to 'size them up' as he puts it."

"Size them up?"

"Yeah, so he can find a weak spot. He's always looking for a weak spot."

Frowning, Gideon says, "Why do I get the feeling my life's about to be hell? I mean, it's already hell, but if hell could get any worse...do you think this is about our punishments?"

Kai nods, "Yeah, I'd bet on it. But look on the bright side, dude. At least it'll be my father making your life hell and not Shelly."

"Aren't you forgetting something? You're in this, too."

"Yeah, but he'll go way easier on me. He thinks I'm a total wuss." Kai grins as he says it, obviously proud of the title.

"Yeah, dude, what's with that?"

"Well, you know how I don't like heights and blood and gore and stuff like that, right?"

"Uh huh."

"When I was a little kid, I'd act like a baby and it got me off the hook all the time."

Gideon wonders if Kai realizes that's why his dad always treats him like a baby.

"I know that look. You think it's lame," Kai says.

"Totally lame."

"Yeah, well it works. Come on, we're going to be late for class."

After school, Gideon tells Kai he's going to walk to his house rather than catch a ride.

"I just need a little time to myself."

Kai shrugs. "Suit yourself."

Gideon watches the Bentley pull away. With all that happened with Ms. Pinkberry, he needs to clear his head and just forget about the whole thing. Put it out of his mind.

Twenty minutes later, Gideon reaches the gate. The guard takes him up to the house in the cart. As they approach the second guard tower, Gideon sees his dad's vintage Jaguar in the Tanaka's driveway. It agitates him. *She drove two miles? It's a miracle she didn't hit anything.*

He hops off the cart.

"Thanks."

The guard heads back down to the first gate.

Gideon stands next to the car, reminiscing about the days he and his dad would take a drive. Just the two of them. His fingertips glide across the back quarter panel of the car. The paint still looks new. *I'll kill her if she damages it. I'm going to kill her anyway, but I'll kill her harder.*

As he reaches the front door, he takes a moment to listen to the waterfall. It's peaceful. It helps calm his nerves. He takes a deep breath and rings the door bell. Oishii answers, wearing her maid uniform. She smiles at him. She looks beautiful, even in her ugly maid frock.

"Hi, Oishii."

"Hello, Gideon. They are expecting you. Won't you please come in?"

She steps back to allow him access into the huge marble entryway. Gideon politely waits for her to close the door so she can escort him.

"Follow me." She winks at him.

Gideon counts the tiny buttons trailing down the back of Oishii's uniform as she leads him to the living room. When he looks up, he finds that everyone in the room is staring at him. His face turns pink. *Shit! Did they all just see me staring at her ass?*

Oishii heads for the kitchen.

Gideon glances at Mr. Tanaka, who's smiling at him.

"Hello, Mr. Tanaka."

"Hello, Gideon."

Looking expectantly at him, Shelly says cooly, "So, what's all this about, Gideon?"

"I have no idea." He takes a seat next to Kai.

Mr. Tanaka speaks first. "Now that we're all here, please, let me explain." He turns his attention to Shelly. "I'd like to thank you, Mrs. Damascus, for accepting my invitation and taking time out of your busy schedule to accommodate this meeting."

Gideon rolls his eyes. *Busy schedule? That's a crock of shit, unless you call being passed out, busy.*

Oishii comes back into the room carrying a tray with two cups of black coffee. Houseki follows behind her carrying a tray with two glasses of lemonade. The girls serve the drinks, then stand against the wall quietly.

Mr. Tanaka leans over to pick up a cup of coffee and shoots a glance at Gideon, who's gritting his teeth.

He hands Shelly the cup as he gives her his best deal-winning smile.

"As I was saying, Mrs. Damascus."

"Please call me Shelly." She bats her eyelashes at him, uncrosses her legs, pretends to dust off her skirt, then re-crosses her legs.

Dirty whore. Gideon glances at Kai who is holding back his laughter.

"Thank you, Shelly, that's very kind of you. Well, this is somewhat embarrassing but recently my maid and cook got into a bit of trouble. Unfortunately, I was going to have to let them go."

Shelly looks up from her coffee in surprise.

"These young women here? No!"

Gideon observes her pointing her index finger directly at the girls. Her rudeness embarrasses him.

"Yes, I'm afraid so," Mr. Tanaka says sternly.

"Whatever did they do?" Shelly toys with a ratty curl on her shoulder, as she pretends to care about their predicament.

"I won't disclose the details. It would be very impolite for me to do so."

"Um, yes, I've heard you Japanese people have a lot of polite customs."

Mr. Tanaka smiles. He refrains from looking over at Gideon for fear he'll burst out laughing.

Gideon looks down at his feet, disgusted. *You Japanese people? God, she's a butthole.*

"That's right. I can see you're not just a beautiful woman but quite inane as well."

"Oh, why thank you, Mr. Tanaka." She waves her hand, pretending to be embarrassed.

Gideon can barely maintain his poker face. *God, she has no idea what it means.*

Shelly leans closer to Mr. Tanaka then plays with the chain around her neck. Gideon imagines himself strangling her with it. He makes a mental note to add that to his list.

Despite finding everything about her extremely offensive, Mr. Tanaka does a good job of pretending to be distracted by her.

"Anyway, getting to the point, our young men, kindly and most chivalrously I might add, offered to take their punishments."

Shelly looks over at the boys. Peering at them suspiciously, she asks sarcastically, "Now why would they want to do a thing like that?"

"To save the girls from being fired, of course," says Mr. Tanaka.

Shifting her eyes sideways Shelly says coolly, "How ever-so-knightly of you two."

Ignoring her sarcasm, Mr. Tanaka says, "Yes, very kind indeed. It shows great character. Normally, I wouldn't allow such a thing, but, as my own son pointed out, we all have a responsibility for charity. He reminded me that charity isn't always just about money."

Leaning over toward him, Shelly pretends to whisper, loud enough so they can all hear.

"What are the punishments?"

"Gideon will only be carrying out menial tasks, I assure you. It's all written here. I certainly wouldn't propose such a thing without your permission, of course. If you would be so kind as to take a moment to read it, my girls would be most grateful to you. There are three places which need signatures, you know, in case of emergency, that kind of thing."

Mr. Tanaka hands a half inch stack of paperwork to Shelly.

She looks down at it and frowns. "There sure are a lot of papers here."

"I apologize for that. My attorney writes this stuff up, and you know how attorneys are. They cover everything from head to toe."

Leaning closer to her, he convincingly adds, "Personally, I think it's just overkill on his part. Simply another way to bill for more hours. I've paid him a fortune over the years."

She smiles and begins to lightly peruse the documents.

The first few paragraphs are just as Mr. Tanaka said, a release allowing him permission to authorize medical attention should Gideon become injured, including giving him medication for his migraines.

"Migraines? Ha, he doesn't get migraines."

The comment surprises Mr. Tanaka. *How could she not know that?*

"Eh, well, attorneys, they cover everything," he says.

She scans further and finds that Gideon will stay at the Tanaka residence for two weeks. He and Kai will be carrying out a list of menial chores for the entire duration of Gideon 's visit.

Shelly picks up the pen and starts to sign but then pauses for a moment. She looks up at Mr. Tanaka.

Immediately, he recognizes the look. *Scheming.* He's made a career of studying people, observing their physical mannerisms, and listening for verbal innuendos.

She twirls the sleek black pen between her fingers.

"Mr. Tanaka, I'm not sure I want to be in a big house all alone by myself for two whole weeks. "

Already a step ahead of her, he replies, "Oh, but you won't. I certainly don't want you to feel lonely Mrs.-- Shelly. My girls will stay with you and tend to your every need."

The girls look at each other, stunned.

Shelly blurts out, "You're giving me your misfits in exchange for my Gideon?!"

The comment infuriates Gideon. Hearing her refer to him as if she owns him makes him fuming mad.

Kai glances at Gideon. His face is red and his temples are bulging. He leans over and whispers, "Dude, weak spot, remember?"

Gideon nods slightly, then forces himself to take a deep breath.

"Well, I wouldn't call them misfits exactly," Mr. Tanaka says. "They're well skilled in massage, they can do your hair and nails quite professionally, and they'll treat you like a celebrity for two whole weeks. They cook and clean. Oishii is very skilled at sewing, should you need any mending done." Mr. Tanaka chuckles, adding, "and they even do windows."

The boys grin at each other. *Hanging out together for two whole weeks!*

They look over at Oishii and Houseki who are clearly disappointed.

"Yes, my girls will tend to your every need. Won't you, ladies?"

"Yes, sir," they say in unison, unenthusiastic.

"I understand Gideon's father passed away several years ago. Forgive me for saying so, but a woman such as yourself-- young, beautiful, feminine-- you shouldn't have the burden of teaching an adolescent male how to be a man. Only a respectable, regimented man can do that." Mr. Tanaka sits back in his chair.

"Father, why don't we just have Shelly stay at --"

Mr. Tanaka puts his hand up to silence Kai.

"I'll send my girls to your residence in two days."

Shelly looks down at her lap for a moment. Quietly she says, "Mr. Tanaka, this is very generous of you, but, well, embarrassing as it is to admit, I'm not sure I have enough money to feed your maids for two whole weeks."

"Oh, not to worry. Forgive me for forgetting to mention..."

He reaches in his sports coat and pulls out a thick envelope and hands it to her.

"Please accept this as compensation for their board and care."

She greedily rips the envelope open.

Gideon wonders what denominations the bills are.

Just as Mr. Tanaka had predicted, Shelly quickly flips to each sticky note where she needs to sign. She doesn't attempt to read any of them. After signing, she hands the paperwork back to him.

Mr. Tanaka carefully folds the pile lengthwise, then places it in the inside pocket of his sports coat. Immediately, he ends the meeting and shows her out.

When he returns to the living room, he takes off his sports coat and loosens his tie. He says something in Japanese to Oishii, and she leaves the room.

Kai speaks first. "I'm sorry, Father, I almost blew it."

"You responded to the signal, that's what's important, son."

Gideon looks at the both of them inquisitively.

Kai explains, "I started to ask father why he didn't just have Shelly stay at one of our hotels. We have a couple of them right here in town."

They own hotels?

Mr. Tanaka says sarcastically, "After meeting her, it's bad enough that she knows where we live. You were right, Gideon, she is a bonafide gold digger."

"You mean a hole digger. She's the biggest brown noser ever."

They all laugh.

Kai informs Gideon about his dad's signal. "If my father puts his hand up like this, we all stop talking immediately."

"That's right," Mr. Tanaka says. "Without having to explain in the middle of a negotiation, it's easiest to give the signal for silence. I can always explain later if necessary."

"Good to know," says Gideon.

Oishii returns with a bottle of saki and five tiny cups.

She fills the cups three-quarters full and Houseki passes them around.

Mr. Tanaka proposes a toast. "Here's to new adventures."

They all clink cups.

"Father, are you really going to send Oishii and Houseki away for two weeks?"

"Yes."

"Who will take care of us? Who will cook, clean, and shop for our food?"

Mr. Tanaka doesn't respond. He stares at his son, waiting for it to sink in.

"That's it, isn't it?" says Gideon. "Dude, don't you get it? Your dad's punishment is making us take Oishii and Houseki's place for the two weeks while they're gone."

"Very good, Gideon."

Kai looks horrified. He scrunches his face and uses his whiny baby voice. "But I don't know how to cook, clean, and shop. I can't do any of that!"

Gideon rolls his eyes.

Mr. Tanaka says sharply, "It's about time you learned, and you will do it!"

Kai cowers.

Mr. Tanaka changes his tone. "Oishii and Houseki will start showing you what to do early tomorrow morning. If you forget or there is something they didn't cover, I'll show you. I've also made a list. You boys have to start learning how to take care of yourselves." Retrieving the list from his front pocket, Mr. Tanaka hands it to Kai.

Kai studies it and groans.

Oishii and Houseki converse in Japanese with Mr. Tanaka. The girls nod and say in unison, "Ms. Shelly," followed by laughter.

Kai hands the list to Gideon. "What stuff do you know how to do around the house?"

Gideon reads the list. "Pretty much everything here, except I don't do too much cooking. That would require going in the kitchen. Shelly goes in there to get ice."

"Okay, I'll learn how to cook and you can clean, shop, and do the laundry," says Kai.

"That's crap, dude, but since you're totally hopeless, I'll do it. I think we should both do the shopping, though."

"Okay, deal."

"Man, if this is all it takes to get me out of the house, I'd do it every day," says Gideon.

"We do other things too," says Oishii.

"Like what?" Kai asks.

"We tend to the Obiats. We bathe them, feed them twice a day, and beat them twice a week," says Houseki.

The hairs on the back of Gideon's neck rise.

Did she just say, "beat the obiats?"

"What? Why do you beat them?" Gideon asks.

"Because--"

"Ahem." Mr. Tanaka frowns at her, then speaks to Houseki in Japanese.

"I will explain it another time," Mr. Tanaka says. "I'll discipline the obiats while Oishii and Houseki are away."

"Wait, you still haven't said why you beat them. Women? Why? Are they bad? Why don't they quit? Where are they? Is that even legal?"

"Yes, Gideon, it is legal. I own them. Enough talk of this. We will discuss this later."

He owns them? Gideon envisions women in compromising positions being whipped with a leather belt. Visions of soft pink flesh and faces of anguish swirl in his head.

"Dude! Are you totally ignoring me?!"

"Huh? No, I was thinking."

Kai starts to repeat whatever he was saying, but Gideon cuts him off. "When you guys beat the obiats, can I watch?"

"Gideon! I said we will discuss it later!" The harshness in Mr. Tanaka's voice makes him jump.

"I certainly won't have any problem strapping you myself if it's warranted."

Strap me?! Holy shit!

Gideon's eyes are as big as saucers.

Mr. Tanaka sets a hand on his shoulder. "I'm sorry, I didn't mean to frighten you. I do tend to yell now and then. If I yell, it's because I want to look out for you boys so you'll be prepared for the real world. You understand, right?"

Gideon nods. He doesn't like Mr. Tanaka yelling at him, but since he gets to stay for two weeks, he'll try not to let it bother him.

"Kai, you'll explain the rules to Gideon and how much respect is expected around here."

"Yes, Father."

Gideon thinks, *Shit, Mr. Tanaka really IS psycho. Everyone should know how to beat their obiats before they go out into the 'real' world?*

"Enough talk. Let's shoot some pool while the girls get dinner ready, shall we?"

Mr. Tanaka stands, looking at them expectantly.

Wishing he could take Gideon to his room to explain his father isn't always a total asshole, Kai says somberly, "Sure."

He gives Gideon a sideways nod toward the game room.

"Right," says Gideon.

Forty-five minutes later, the three men have moved past the earlier conversation. They're joking and laughing amongst each other.

Mr. Tanaka brings up the fact that he hasn't ever taken Kai to a theme park.

"Have you been to an amusement park, Gideon?"

"No, Shelly would say it was a waste of money."

"I'd like you boys to discuss which parks you'd like to visit and I'll see what I can work out."

As they play another round of pool, Kai and Gideon discuss the different theme parks. They agree on five of them.

Oishii enters. Having changed back into her starched apron and her stilettos, she says, "Dinner is ready, gentlemen."

In the dining room, Houseki is waiting to serve the food. She has a sad look on her face.

"Don't be unhappy, my pet. It's only for two weeks."

"Yes, sir," she says, dismally.

"Since you girls will be gone for a while, why don't you let Kai and Gideon entertain you tonight?"

The boys beam at each other.

"Really, Father?" Kai asks.

Mr. Tanaka smiles. "Considering you boys will be filling in for them for the next two weeks, it seems like a nice thing to do."

"Thank you, Mr. Tanaka. That's so cool of you."

Several hours later, Gideon pulls the blanket off the bed and kicks the sheet all the way down to the end. The cool pillow feels good behind his warm neck and wet curls. Across the room, Kai is snoring, even though the girls only left five minutes ago.

Despite lying in his own sweat, Gideon can still smell Houseki. The scent of hibiscus mixed with her sweet juices from straddling his face still lingers. He made sure to get his fill since there was no telling when he'd have the opportunity to have sex with her again. *I should take a shower.* Being too exhausted, his body is unwilling to budge. He gazes into the darkness until his eyelids drop and sleep takes over.

Mr. Tanaka sits back in his office chair, breathless. He purposefully delays himself gratification as he watches his monitor. The camera in Kai's room is perfectly hidden in the form of a sprinkler head right above Gideon. He zooms in. He touches himself some more and zooms the camera out to see Gideon's nude body blanketed by the moonlight.

What is it about him? He thinks about his conversations with Gideon. It stands out how unassuming, yet intentional Gideon is about everything he says and does.

He controls his own thoughts, rather than his thoughts controlling him. He doesn't conform.

And there it is, his answer, *Gideon is a challenge.*

Mr. Tanaka zooms in on his face, close enough to see the beads of sweat on Gideon's upper lip. Zooming the camera lens out slowly, he strokes himself, firmer, faster, this time with more intention. As Gideon's body comes into view again, the storm musters up inside him, and he makes no attempt to suppress it. The surge overcomes him, tearing through his body, causing the muscles in his abdomen to involuntarily flex and shudder. It's been a long time since he came so deeply. He sits back in his chair, feeling relaxed, satisfied. *Finally, someone worthy of my attention...*

POND OF ENLIGHTENMENT

Mr. Tanaka takes the middle seat in front of the video console. Kai and Gideon sit to either side of him.

"Father, I didn't know you play video games."

"There's only one game I play. This one." Mr. Tanaka holds up a mysterious black box. There's a silver dragon on the front.

"Why only that one, Father?"

"It represents a rivalry between myself and an old enemy. It's one of a kind. I wrote the story, then had it developed into a video game."

"You wrote the story?" asks Gideon.

"That's right."

"How come I never knew this?" Kai says. "There are so many things you've never told me."

"What's the story about?" asks Gideon.

"It's about a young man named Horosha, which means 'wanderer'. He's a bit like you boys. He doesn't yet understand his full potential. He only knows he has a desire to get to The Pond of Enlightenment."

"What's so special about the pond?" asks Kai.

"It's been said that it opens the third eye to one's own self-awareness. For those who are destined for pure good, the pond sends up a golden shell. Only with the golden shell can the wanderer drink from the pond and receive its gifts."

"What if they got on their bellies and put their face in it or drank from their hands?" asks Gideon.

"Legend has it that many have tried. They suffered burns and the effects of poisonous water, and later died. Only with a golden shell can the water be safely consumed."

Curious Kai asks, "What happens if Horosha acquires the golden shell and drinks from the pond?"

"The water bestows great gifts upon those who consume it. It will turn him into a great warrior. Mind you, no one is even sure if anyone has ever achieved it. There've been rumors that people have done it, but no one has ever actually seen anyone accomplishing it. Villagers have boasted about finding it, only to die shortly afterward."

"Cool," says Gideon.

"The character Horosha is a brave man, but a wise one. Wise enough to recognize the journey is very dangerous. Most likely lethal. He weighs the good and the bad. If he fails, he decides he won't return to face the shame of defeat. He'll perish in solitude. But, if he succeeds, he may find his purpose and become the greatest warrior ever to live. So, he decides he must go."

Gideon grins. "Sounds awesome. Let's play."

"Not so fast. There are many unexpected obstacles along the way that I need to clue you into. Evil influencers will try to tempt Horosha to distract him from accomplishing his goal."

"Distractions?" Kai asks, "what distractions?"

"He's put into precarious situations where dark forces attack him in the middle of the street. At times there will be children playing, caught in the crossfire. Horosha will have to make hard choices. He can use the children as human shields to save himself or he can use himself to protect them, taking severe blows along the way. I will warn you that this game will test your character. It can make you humble, humiliated, ashamed, or proud, depending on what kind of a man you are. Since I've played the game before, I have a slight edge over you boys, which is why I'm giving you some insight to help you."

"Are there any cheat codes?" asks Kai.

Mr. Tanaka yells, "There is no cheating in my game!"

Kai cowers.

Softening his tone, Mr. Tanaka says, "No, son, there are no cheats. I'll offer a word of advice. No matter how hard you try, you cannot save them all. This game shows the worst of humanity, in hopes of seeking out the best. That's just how the game goes."

"What did you learn about yourself the first time you played it, Mr. Tanaka?"

Staring into Gideon's eyes, Mr. Tanaka smiles and says, "I'll have to think about it and get back to you."

Gideon's pretty sure after having said all that, Mr. Tanaka doesn't want to say he's just another asshole like everyone else. Leaning over, Gideon gives Kai a sardonic grin. "Game on."

Kai sneers at him in fun. "Yeah, game on."

Mr. Tanaka looks at Kai and adds, "One last thing. This is a very graphic game. If for any reason you want to stop, push the purple button on your controller. It will suspend the game for thirty seconds which will give you a moment to decide whether or not you want to stop until another time. I sometimes use it to take a short break."

"Why are you looking at me? I'm not a baby!"

"I certainly meant nothing in particular. I just thought I'd throw it out there. I'm only looking at you, because, well, because Gideon is a guest and it would be impolite to single him out." He looks over at Gideon and winks.

Gideon nods. "Thanks, Mr. Tanaka."

A short movie begins, telling the story of Horosha and his quest. The graphics are so vivid that the characters appear to jump off the screen and back into the game again.

The narrator explains Horosha's treacherous journey ahead. He must enter the gates and travel through Dragon City, cross the poison ruby marshes, hike over the black hills, and head into the jade forest.

"Once there, he will face the guardians of the Pond of Enlightenment," the narrator warns. "Trust no one but yourself."

The screen splits into three panels. Each player's Horosha stands in front of a metal gate. Sprawled across it, an iron dragon holds a scorched banner in its mouth labeled 'Dragon City'. Beyond the gate, each player has the same view. The street is lined with cars and shopping vendors.

Mr. Tanaka gives the boys a couple of minutes to get used to the buttons on the controllers. He watches Kai's Horosha jump up and down, move side to side, throw punches, and do side-kicks.

On Gideon's screen, Horosha has climbed up the gate and is using a shell to pry off and steal the fire opals from the eyes of the iron dragon.

Mr. Tanaka laughs. "Ah, so you're a thief, eh?"

Gideon shrugs, "Figured I might trade them for a weapon."

"Very wise indeed. I've never stolen them before."

Both Kai and Mr. Tanaka steal the eyes off their dragons as well.

"Is everyone ready?" asks Mr. Tanaka.

"Ready," says Gideon.

"Good to go," says Kai.

The game begins. As each Horosha enters the city he is immediately approached by a beautiful Japanese woman, offering a tour of the city. Both boys attempt to walk away, but Kai's Horosha #1, and Gideon's Horosha #3, start having sex with her.

"Hey," Gideon says, "my controller isn't responding."

"Mine neither," says Kai.

Mr. Tanaka pauses the game.

"Oh, I forgot to mention that Horosha isn't always controllable. At times he does what he wants. If he wants to have sex, he does. There are small parts of the game where he thinks for himself."

Gideon asks, "How can you tell that he's thinking for himself?"

"You'll see tiny pepper-like flashes above his head. Right there, see?"

"Oh yeah, okay. Got it."

"If you see a quick yellow flash over his head, it means you have five seconds before he starts thinking on his own. That's your opportunity to fight before your Horosha begins to think for himself."

"Can you back up the game to where the gate opens, Father?"

Mr. Tanaka backs it up and restarts the game at the gate.

Gideon's Horosha #3 runs around the woman. She chases him down a few streets. He finds a grenade on the seat of a jeep and tosses it behind him, blowing her up. He barely escapes the fallout from the explosion. He sees a church where he decides to seek refuge.

At the steps of the church, Mr. Tanaka's Horosha #2 is waiting. His Horosha got away from the woman by snapping her neck. Kai's Horosha #1 reaches the steps, looking thrashed. The woman in the street punched him in the face, giving him a black eye, then she stole his opals.

Horosha #2 bangs on the door. A monk opens a small window in the door. Gideon's Horosha #3 gives him an opal and he invites them inside. The monk explains no one expects to find much of anything in a place of holiness. He shows them a room with a cache of weapons. In the corner of the room, a fat monk sits at a small table of food. He's lecturing a skinny boy about not bringing him enough butter. He whops the boy on the back of his head.

"What a jerk," says Kai.

Gideon giggles.

The three Horosha's stock up on guns, knives, and small explosives. Before leaving they're blessed by the two monks. Kai shoots the fat one. Mr. Tanaka and Gideon look over at him.

Kai shrugs. "He was mean."

As they leave the church, Gideon's Horosha #3 is attacked in the street by three young men. He kills all of them.

During the next round of altercations, Gideon stabs a street vendor who attacks him with a broken bottle. The vendor isn't dead, just seriously wounded. Gideon tries to finish him off by twisting the knife. A pop-up window appears. The vendor gives him information about the next upcoming traps. He twists the knife again and the vendor tells him ways to avoid other traps.

Gideon attacks several innocent street vendors, inflicting pain on them to obtain information about the best routes to take, where to find more weapons, secret passages, and how to avoid some altercations altogether.

Occasionally, Mr. Tanaka finds himself watching what's happening on Gideon's screen. He's impressed. When his game developer first gave him the finished product, it took him a few times playing to discover the hidden torture tricks. No other game has this form of hidden tricks, yet Gideon stumbled onto it quickly. *What does it say about him?*

Kai's Horosha #1 repeatedly hides, gets caught, then gets the crap beat out of him.

He's been killed twice, each time landing him back at square one. As he plays, he physically cringes at the violent images. It would only be a matter of time before he bails out of the game. Mr. Tanaka glances at Kai's screen. He can't help think that while his son may not have the stomach for violence, he certainly has the kindness of someone worthy of the Pond of Enlightenment.

A moment later all of their screens freeze. Horosha #1 is flashing purple.

Kai looks down at his controller. "Father, would it be all right if I go play another video game?"

"Sure, son. This game isn't entertaining to everyone."

Turning to him, Kai says, "I hope you're not disappointed. It's just that slash and dash really isn't my thing. I'm more into Fighter Pilots."

Mr. Tanaka smiles at him. "Play whatever is enjoyable. I'm not disappointed or offended."

Gideon looks at Kai. "Fighter pilot is cool, dude. I suck at that game. I get shot down every time."

Kai smiles. "I know, right? I've got the top score. When you guys are done slashing each other, let's play pool."

"Sounds good," says Gideon.

Mr. Tanaka nods. "Good plan."

Kai goes over to the cockpit booth. Gideon and Mr. Tanaka resume their game.

Horosha #2 and #3 are pretty even. Twenty minutes later, they're both still alive. They fought their way out of Dragon City and are crossing the alligator filled swamp water in the Ruby Marshes. They periodically see each other through the reeds.

Another short movie plays, setting up the next level.

Gideon asks Mr. Tanaka if he can pause the screen and go back to the last scene in Dragon City.

Mr. Tanaka backs the game up.

"Can you stop it at that last fight scene, at the close up of the dead girl?"

Mr. Tanaka rewinds the game.

Gideon walks up to the t.v. screen. "There, stop. Back up a little, stop, right there."

Gideon studies the image. "This has been messed with."

Mr. Tanaka is stunned Gideon noticed it so fast.

"What do you mean?"

Gideon sits back down, "Did you see the flicker right before you stopped the video? I think an image was spliced in. Offset slightly, which causes that flicker."

"What are you saying?"

"I'm saying some kind of art work or changes were made right here. An add-in maybe."

Mr. Tanaka has a salacious grin. "Aren't you the perceptive one?"

Gideon isn't sure if he's complimenting him or if he thinks he's criticizing his game.

"I wasn't being critical. I'm just amazed how real and--"

Mr. Tanaka raises his hand to cut him off. "I was actually being quite serious. The fact that you picked up on that exact cut is very perceptive."

He lowers his voice. "You're correct, it is a paste-in. A photo. But it's not something I want to share with anyone else. Do you understand?"

Gideon nods. He wonders, *who took it? How did Mr. Tanaka get it?*

Mr. Tanaka resumes the game.

A few minutes later Gideon whispers, "May I see it?"

"See what?"

"The photo."

Mr. Tanaka smiles. *Finally...something to manipulate him.*

"Are you asking to see all the pictures or just that one?"

Gideon's face lights up.

"You have more?"

Mr. Tanaka leans over, whispering, "I have video footage as well."

Gideon stares wide-eyed at him.

"No one else can know. It's disturbing, but I think you can handle it. We can discuss it after Kai's asleep. I'll send one of the girls to get you."

Gideon nods. Questions fill his head.

Mr. Tanaka resumes the game and fast-forwards it to where they were, prior to rewinding.

Five minutes later, Gideon hits the pause button. "Can I save my game? You know, so I can continue where I left off later?"

"Certainly. You're not bored with my game already, are you?"

"No. It's awesome. It's getting late and Kai still wants to play pool..." He stretches and winks.

Mr. Tanaka chuckles. "Okay. Let's all play pool."

UNDERSTANDING

Stretched out on the grass with the sun in his face, he stirs. The water running in the creek sounds peaceful. The mild afternoon breeze rustles the tree branches above him. Gideon opens his sleepy eyes to find Snow White sitting next to him, silently reading her book. Her black hair glistens like a raven in the sunshine.

As he reaches for her, she turns her head to look at him. He expects to see Snow's round blue eyes, but the eyes looking back at him are hazel green, almond shaped. He sits up. "Mom?"

As her gentle hand touches his shoulder, everything goes dark.

"Mom?!"

Oishii stands over him in the moonlight. A familiar pain sits in Gideon's chest. He realizes he's been dreaming. Oishii must have been sent to wake him.

"I'm sorry, Gideon. It's only me," she whispers.

"Oishii, what time is it?"

"One a.m., sir. My master sent me to fetch you. He said you wouldn't mind."

Gideon reaches for his shirt. He pulls it over his head, then picks up his sneakers and quietly tiptoes out of Kai's room.

Oishii waits while he ties his shoes, then leads him up to the third floor.

Moments later, they arrive in front of a black, highly polished door. Spanning across it is a green and blue dragon tail. The door handle is forged into a dragon claw. Oishii picks up a receiver hanging on the wall.

"Yes, sir, Mr. Gideon is here. Goodnight."

There's a high-pitched buzz and Oishii pulls the ornate handle, holding the door open for Gideon.

"Goodnight, Gideon."

"Aren't you coming?"

"No, sir. My master requested to see you in his room alone."

This is his bedroom?

"Oishii, Mr. Tanaka is safe, right?"

She frowns. "Sorry?"

"I'm safe hanging out with him alone, right? He won't hurt me or anything?"

She giggles. "Not unless you want him to."

Gideon steps inside the entrance to the bedroom. The floor is slightly raised. The furniture is massive. Everything in the room is charcoal grey except the black dragon statues.

Not seeing Mr. Tanaka, he calls out, "Hello, Mr. Tanaka?"

"I'm back here, Gideon. Come on back."

He walks through the bedroom into a hallway lined wall to wall, floor to ceiling, in a deep blue-gray stone. Pebble-sized crystallized white pits and long threads of copper run through it in every direction. It makes him think of meteors flying across a galaxy. He's awed by it.

"Back here, Gideon."

He continues into an adjoining room. There's a giant black statue in the middle of the room.

"Whoa!"

It's close to fifteen feet tall. Three of the walls surrounding it have floor to ceiling highly polished built-in black lacquered cabinets and drawers. The fourth wall is made of glass, overlooking the landscape.

He walks up to the statue to get a closer look. It's made of solid black marble.

"Do you like it?"

Gideon turns to see Mr. Tanaka wearing a black jogging suit.

"Yeah. It's cool."

"I debated whether or not to put him up here. I'm glad I did. He works well with the room."

"How did you get him up here?"

"He was brought in by crane before the walls were built."

"You built this mansion?"

"That's right."

"So, where did the behemoth come from?"

"That 'behemoth,' as you put it, is Poseidon, God of the Sea. The statue is carbon dated to 450 BC. It was a gift from my father, when I took over my first fleet."

"Your first fleet?"

"Yes, I ship goods all over the world by ocean liners. That's what I do. My company is the largest import/exporter in the world."

Gideon wonders why Kai never told him about this.

"What type of goods do you ship?"

"How did I know you were going to ask me that? Such a curious guy for your age."

"Sorry, I didn't mean--"

"Let's have a drink, shall we?"

"Uh, a drink? I'm underage, but you already know that…"

Mr. Tanaka chuckles and pours a light brown liquid into two fancy fat round glasses. He hands one to Gideon.

"I think if you're man enough to have sex with my housemaids, you're man enough to join me for a drink, don't you?"

Gideon nods and nervously gulps down his entire drink.

Mr. Tanaka smiles at him as if he'd just done something humorous.

"What? What's so funny?"

As he refills Gideon's glass he says, "This is a sipping liqueur. It's meant to be savored a bit. If you down it too fast, you're going to get very drunk rather quickly. Possibly very sick, and we certainly wouldn't want that."

"Right, no, sorry."

Mr. Tanaka sips his Amaretto. Gideon observes him as he holds the liquid in his mouth, hesitating, before swallowing it. He motions for Gideon to follow him over to the chairs by the fire. There's a small table between them.

"Kick off your shoes. Make yourself comfortable."

Kicking off his sneakers, Gideon takes a seat.

Mr. Tanaka observes Gideon as he takes his second sip of Amaretto, allowing the sweet almond liquid to sit on his tongue. As it slowly rolls off the edges, Gideon swallows.

"See?" Mr. Tanaka says. "Some things are just better enjoyed slowly."

Gideon nods. "It burns my throat, but it's good."

"Indeed." *A pinch of ecstasy does that.*

It isn't particularly necessary to drug Gideon, but a teensy bit of the drug would make him more malleable.

"Firsts, in almost every way, are always the best, wouldn't you agree?"

"If they're good, yes," says Gideon.

"You tend to be very decisive with your responses."

"It's all people want." Gideon takes another sip, mindful to hold the liquid on his tongue.

"Why do you suppose that is?"

Swallowing, he replies, "Well, people see me as a kid, right?"

"For the most part, yes."

Gideon sets his drink on the table as he explains, "When adults ask kids questions, they just want a straight answer without any hoopla behind it."

Amused, Mr. Tanaka smiles at him. "That's very insightful of you. When I was your age, the younger generation was seen, but rarely heard. If my father asked a question, I tended to keep my replies short. If there was 'hoopla' behind it, as you put it, he would have assumed I was lying."

"I think it's the same today." Feeling more relaxed, Gideon asks, "Can we talk about the video game?"

Mr. Tanaka leans forward. He needs to solidify an agreement between them before the alcohol and drugs kick in, otherwise Gideon might not remember making it.

"We need to have an understanding between us. I'll tell you what you want to know about the game, but I need to know that I have your trust."

Gideon nods.

"Also, in the course of our private discussions, nothing is ever to be repeated. Never. I feel you can be trusted, otherwise you wouldn't still be here."

"I'm not a blabber. You can count on me, Mr. Tanaka."

"My trust doesn't come without obligations. Under my roof, you must agree to do exactly as I tell you. In return, you'll be extended all the comforts of life, well, with the exception of my pets, that is. If you can agree to those terms, we can be friends. If not, I'll need to re-evaluate whether or not I can trust you."

Mr. Tanaka holds his hand out to him.

It occurs to Gideon this is more of an ultimatum than an option. If he doesn't shake, it will jeopardize his friendship with Kai. Other than home, this is the only place he has to go. *There's always food in this house.* He'd be stupid to risk losing it.

"Agreed," he says. He shakes Mr. Tanaka's hand.

"Excellent! Just a word of advice, don't ever break that commitment. There will be grave consequences if you do."

Commitment? Gideon finds Mr. Tanaka intimidating, but as long as he does what he's told, he figures it'll be okay. He has no intention of ever betraying a total psycho.

Mr. Tanaka hands Gideon his drink. "To friendship and solidifying our mutual understanding."

"To friendship," says Gideon. He's fuzzy on the solidification part, but he'd just make sure to keep his commitment. Whatever that was. He drinks to the toast.

Mr. Tanaka studies him. *He has no idea what he's getting into. I'll need to spell it out for him.*

"Just do what I say, keep our secrets, and you'll be fine."

Gideon nods. "Secrets, got it."

There's a moment of silence as they both attempt to read one another.

Gideon glances around the room. "There's quite a lot of artwork in here."

"Each one is hand-picked from a trip or was given to me as a gift."

"Which one is your favorite?"

"This one." Mr. Tanaka points to a black and white creation hanging fifteen feet to his right.

Gideon gets up and walks over to it. On the left side of the canvas a thin line starts. It seems to move to the right, in a soft waving motion until, a quarter of the way across, it curves around, passing over itself. As it does, the line becomes thicker. It continues right and curves around again. Each time it does, the line increases in thickness. As it reaches the center, it gets more and more convoluted. The curves change from soft rolling bends to hard rigid angles. Three quarters of the way across the canvas it forms a thick angry mass. By the time it reaches the far right, it evolves into a thick black blob.

"What's it called?"

Mr. Tanaka gets up and stands next to him.

"It's called, 'Innocence Lost to Obligation.' It reminds us that in succumbing to the responsibilities of life, one can lose a sense of tenderness and joy. We become more and more overwhelmed, bitter, and eventually die."

"I didn't know art could say all that."

The more he studies it, the more it seems to mimic his life. *It all starts out so innocent, yet ends so dark.*

Mr. Tanaka notices the intense look on Gideon's face.

"I believe I agreed to show you something. Follow me."

SECRET ROOM

Mr. Tanaka escorts Gideon through a narrow hallway which leads to a small room. Other than a chandelier casting soft light over the emerald green walls, there's a miniature framed print of a flame, hanging on the wall.

Mr. Tanaka lifts it, exposing a keypad. He enters his code. The wall slides open, revealing a dimly lit hallway.

Gideon leans inside. The hairs on the back of his neck stand up.

With a sardonic grin, Mr. Tanaka says, "You first."

Gideon hesitates, then steps inside. Mr. Tanaka follows. He pushes a button and the wall closes.

"Now you're at my mercy," he says jokingly.

Gideon chuckles nervously.

He follows Mr. Tanaka down a set of stairs. They enter a room where the walls are decorated in blood red wallpaper. Gideon moves closer to study the embossed velvet images of dragons, nude men and women carrying water jugs and baskets.

The dragons wear collars, as do the humans. Chains are attached to the bands on their wrists. It occurs to Gideon there's nothing specific to show whether the dragons are captive or the men and women.

He walks along the wall looking for clues. He finds a dragon carrying a whip. As he walks around the room inspecting the wall paper, he finds two other dragons also carrying whips.

As Mr. Tanaka refreshes their drinks he asks, "Tell me, Gideon, what's going on here?"

"The humans are enslaved to the dragons. Feeding them, I believe."

"Very good."

Gideon glances at the shackles hanging on the opposite wall. Butterflies stir in his belly. *Are those for decoration?*

They move to the far end of the room to a red velvet couch. It appears to match the wallpaper perfectly. In front of it is a gold lacquered coffee table.

Mr. Tanaka sets the drinks down and motions for Gideon to sit. He sets a large black box on the table and retrieves several photos from it. He lays out pictures of a nude Japanese woman.

Gideon leans in to get a better look. The pictures are arousing. Upon close inspection, he sees the woman has undergone a transformation of sorts. In the first pictures, she's a normal young girl who by Gideon's guesstimate would be in her late teens to early twenties.

Both arms are tied over her head. Her long black hair covers her chest and frames her abdomen. Her face appears calm, unafraid.

Over the series of pictures, she's older and her figure is altered.

Her breasts are too large for her frame. Her mouth is fuller. Her eyes are larger. She's strange, yet stunning. She looks like a real-life doll.

"Who is she?" asks Gideon.

"She's the daughter of my former nemesis. He was killed in an unfortunate accident."

"What kind of accident?"

"He accidentally fell out of a twenty-story hospital building after having bypass surgery."

"You mean he actually got out of bed and fell out of a window?"

Mr. Tanaka tilts his head back and forth nonchalantly, "Um hmm. Something like that. Unfortunately for him, his daughter was in the hospital room visiting him at the time. I adopted her at the moment of impact. It was my legal right as her godfather."

"Where was her mother?"

"Drunk at home."

Gideon sniggers. "That sounds familiar."

Mr. Tanaka hands Gideon his drink. They each take a sip.

"I enjoyed sending her mother pictures of her daughter's new look, along with my associates taking advantage of her new assets."

"That's kind of mean, isn't it?"

Reminiscing, Mr. Tanaka says, "Yesss."

Noticing the salacious grin on his face, Gideon surmises that whatever it was Mr. Tanaka hated about the man, he derived great pleasure from rubbing it in his widow's face and taking it out on their daughter.

Spreading out the next set of pictures, Mr. Tanaka observes Gideon intently.

Gideon leans in closer.

The same girl is red in areas all over her body. There are images of her being spanked, belted, and slapped. In one photo, she's been hog tied with clothes pins attached to each nipple. Gideon can tell by her expression, it's agonizing.

Here we go, hardcore.

Mr. Tanaka scoops up the remaining pictures from the box. He hands Gideon his glass.

Gideon sips as Mr. Tanaka slowly lays out all but two photos.

The first one shows the girl with a small cut on her neck. Her breasts are bound with ropes. Her face is expressionless.

"She looks unafraid. Was she drugged?"

Nodding, Mr. Tanaka mumbles, "Opium."

By the end of the stack, the woman is dead. Gideon stares at the photos, attempting to memorize every detail before they go back in the box. He holds his drink in his lap, hoping to hide the erection under his pajamas. The pictures are the most provocative thing he's ever seen.

"If you think back, you'll recall the murder of the hooker in the street in my video game."

Mr. Tanaka hands him two remaining photographs. "These are the overlays used for that murder scene."

Peering at them, Gideon says, "Unbelievable. Who would have thought?"

"Memorializing her in something I could revisit seemed fitting, and my I.T. guy is very good at what he does."

"Do you suppose you're the only one he's done this for?"

"Definitely not."

Gathering up the pictures, Mr. Tanaka sets them in the box.

"Do you trust me, Gideon?"

Tilting his head, Gideon replies, "Uh…I guess so."

"There's something else I want to show you."

Gideon follows Mr. Tanaka over to the credenza where the shackles are hanging on the wall. As Mr. Tanaka opens a drawer, Gideon sees several different types of hand cuffs.

He steps closer to look at them.

Mr. Tanaka glances down at Gideon's hands. Holding them over his groin, he's attempting to hide his excitement.

"Don't be embarrassed about your body responding. That's not something you can control."

Gideon blushes and looks up at the shackles hanging on the wall.

"Excellent choice."

Mr. Tanaka reaches over and pulls them off the wall.

What?!

"Uh no, I wasn't choosing anything."

"You were, you just didn't know it. Hold out your hands."

Mr. Tanaka stands expectantly in front of him, holding open the cuffs.

"After showing me those pictures of what you did to little Ms. Slashed Potatoes, you want me to let you shackle me?!"

The smirk on Mr. Tanaka's face tells him that's exactly what he wants.

Gideon reconciles it quickly in his head. If Mr. Tanaka had wanted him dead, he could have done it already. This could also be a test since he did agree to do whatever he asked. After much silence, Gideon slowly raises his wrists.

In an instant, Mr. Tanaka snaps on the cuffs and attaches them to a hook, which seems to have appeared out of nowhere.

Gideon feels his arms quickly being hoisted up over his head. *What's happening?* Confused, he looks to Mr. Tanaka, who is holding a remote control.

Toying with him, Mr. Tanaka pushes a button, putting slack on the chain, then tightening it, bringing Gideon up on his tiptoes.

Feeling his heart race, Gideon laughs nervously, "Whoa, okay, you got me. I'm freaking out a bit."

"Is that what you're doing?" Mr. Tanaka chuckles at how gullible and easy it is to manipulate Gideon. He notices the hairs are standing up on Gideon's arms. *Perhaps he is freaking out, but by his enormous hard-on, he also likes it.*

"I'm just messing with you, dude." Mr. Tanaka lowers Gideon down slightly so that he's standing back on his feet.

"Oh, man! You scared the crap out of me for a second."

158

Expecting Mr. Tanaka to undo the cuffs, Gideon stands motionless and waits. When no move is made to remove them, he realizes Mr. Tanaka doesn't intend to.

The hard-on poking against Gideon's pajamas makes him feel incredibly embarrassed and vulnerable. He looks down at himself and unsuccessfully tries to will his cock to behave.

Mr. Tanaka looks as if he's entertained by it all.

Gideon looks up at him and says, "Yeah, sorry, it never does what I want it to."

"Still embarassed about your body, are you?"

Gideon blushes and watches as Mr. Tanaka paces the floor back and forth.

He seems to be deciding something. Maybe he didn't intend for it to go this far. Or maybe he just wants me to think that. Kai's right. His dad's a total mind fuck.

Holding Gideon's drink to his lips, Mr. Tanaka says, "Drink!"

Gideon giggles. *The gruff act is hilarious.* He takes a sip, swallowing quickly.

Mr. Tanaka frowns. "Let's try this again. Sip, but this time, 'savor' it."

"Oh yeah, sorry." He takes another sip and holds it in his mouth before letting it ooze down his gullet.

Gideon notices the women on the wallpaper are watching him with curiosity. They're moving slightly.

"Would you like to see the video of her end, Gideon?"

Gideon's cock bobs up and down. *Damn, quit it!*

He'd like to see the video, but he wonders what it's going to cost him.

Swallowing hard, he manages a weak, "Yes."

Mr. Tanaka turns his back to him and starts digging in a drawer.

"What would you do if I gave you your own girl to make your own movie?"

Gideon's cock involuntarily bobs up and down again. *Stop it!*

He envisions a naked, helpless girl, who he'd fuck, slap, and then slash up.

"You mean to make my own snuff film?"

Slipping something in his pocket, Mr. Tanaka closes the drawer. When he turns around, Gideon notices he's no longer the only one with a sizeable erection.

"That's a vulgar term. Please don't repeat it."

"Sorry."

"I'll show you the video from tonight's pictures, if you agree to let me try something on you."

"Do what? Why? Will it hurt?"

Mr. Tanaka smiles. The word 'will' is a good indication that he could actually get him to do it.

"No, it won't hurt. Just wear it for thirty seconds, nothing more."

"What is it? Uh, you know I'm not gay, right?"

"Watching the way you screw my servants, I'm pretty sure you're not. Nor am I. If I was, I'd have male servants, wouldn't I?"

Gideon sees the male servants on the wall paper nodding in agreement.

"Good point."

"What I want you to try on is called a cock ring, but it won't hurt, I promise. How about it? I'll play the video for you, if you try it on. You'll only have it on for half a minute."

Contemplating it, Gideon's curious to know what it's for, but it's too embarassing to admit.

Enthusiastically, Mr. Tanaka says, "This is your one chance to see a real murder!" He frowns slightly, saying, "If there is no trust between us, I might reconsider your sincerity about our agreement this evening."

Aw, fuck! The food is so good here, too.

"No chance you could be wrong about it hurting?"

"I give you my word."

Gideon nods. "Okay."

Mr. Tanaka takes a sip of his drink.

"So, are you going to release me so I can try on this thing-a-ma-jig?"

Holding Gideon's glass to his lips, Mr. Tanaka replies, "Oh no, it's much more fun keeping you in the dark."

The lascivious look on his face causes the hairs to stand up on the back of Gideon's neck.

Using his remote, Mr. Tanaka dims the light. A screen lowers from the ceiling.

Gideon chuckles. Suddenly, this seems all too prepared. He wonders if he's been bamboozled.

"So how many others have you lured down here and chained up?"

Mr. Tanaka doesn't respond. He brings a small stool and black leather box, and sets it next to Gideon's feet.

"I'm not the first person you've brought down here, right?" Gideon's words are a little jumbled. He looks over at the wallpaper.

The women are now talking in cliques, holding their baskets over their hips.

"So, what was in that drink?"

"Actually, other than myself, you're the only person to enter this room."

Really?

The males on the wall are 'high-fiving' each other, and glancing over their shoulder at him. Gideon's sure they're talking about him. *Assholes.*

He glances down at Mr. Tanaka. Boozy, he says, "The humans on the wall are all talking about me. Slacking off. Do you suppose the dragons will eat them?"

Looking up at them, Gideon sees they're all giving him the finger.

Mr. Tanaka chuckles to himself. *Such a lightweight.*

"What's in that box?"

"In Japan as far back as the 1700's, there were entertainers known as geishas."

"Those ladies who paint their faces white?"

"That's right."

"You have a geisha in there?"

Half stoned out of his mind and still such a wit.

While checking the contents of the box Mr. Tanaka says, "The first geisha were actually men. They performed for wealthy households who maintained servants for a variety of things."

"Fuck buddies?" Gideon laughs as he says it.

"Well, certainly they had servants for that, but these were geisha, not courtesans."

Gideon slurs, "What's a courtesan?"

"Courtesans are basically prostitutes. Throughout history, they've been both male and female. Nowadays, wealthy households have courtesans who in a sense fulfill the role of a geisha but also are expected to perform sex."

"Are they gay?"

Mr. Tanaka shakes his head. "No, they're educated, talented men who have real skills. They also have sexual encounters with their employers. Wealthy employers such as myself don't discriminate between men or women. We simply expect to be served."

"In that case, I want to be rich too. Actually, I'm pretty sure I am, I just don't have any money."

The comment makes Mr. Tanaka chuckle.

"The greatest pleasures in life, Gideon, have nothing to do with money. It only makes it easier to access things. In reality, having things happen organically is far more pleasurable."

Having a hard time keeping up, Gideon asks, "You still haven't said why you want me to wear whatever it is."

"I'm only curious as to how your body responds to it. Everyone responds differently."

"You've put this thing on other people?"

"Not this one in particular, but yes, I have put many things on both men and women over the years, just for the curiosity of knowing how their body responds. Aren't you somewhat curious?"

Gideon nods drunkenly. Everyone in the wallpaper gives him the thumbs up, egging him on.

"Wealthy men appreciate the company and intelligence of their own kind. Contrary to popular belief, if two men enjoy making each other feel good, that doesn't make them gay."

"Not to sound bored or anything, but are you going to start the video soon?"

Pointing the remote control at the screen, Mr. Tanaka starts the video. An image of an ornate dagger appears on screen. The black handle is carved into the image of a dragon. Gideon tries to focus as introductions start to roll.

Removing the measurement strap from its box, Mr. Tanaka sanitizes it with a small vial of disinfectant. He sets it down on a silk scarf to dry. It will allow him to measure Gideon's girth for the implement he intends him to wear later on.

"Getting back to courtesans, think about it, have you ever met a female you wanted to talk to, who's as intelligent as yourself?"

Shaking his head, Gideon says, "No, the girls at school are stuck-up bitches. They only hang out in their own circles."

Gideon turns his attention to the video. As the storyline starts, he sees a younger Mr. Tanaka taking his time seducing the young woman from the photos.

With Gideon completely engrossed, Mr. Tanaka begins to bestow upon him his first taste of erotic vulnerability. He pulls down Gideon's pajama bottoms, unveiling his engorged cock.

He glances at Gideon's flushed face and says matter of factly, "I don't want to spill oil on your pajamas." Pouring a half teaspoon of oil between his palms, he gently spreads it over Gideon.

Gideon gasps.

In a nonchalant tone Mr. Tanaka adds, "I'm prepping the shaft so you don't get chafed."

Gideon tries to ignore the sensation of Mr. Tanaka's warm hands, but he's hornier than ever.

"In my opinion, Gideon, women have an inferior intelligence. I enjoy conversations with men far more. Women are so…scattered. This is why elites in my circle have both men and women servants."

Gideon involuntarily squirms, trying to ignore his neediness.

"This circle…uh…do they all have human pets?"

"Yes."

Fastening the cock ring sizer around Gideon's erection, Mr. Tanaka makes a mental note of the measurement. He unlatches it, lengthens the strap, and reattaches it around Gideon's cock and testicles.

The sensation further heightens Gideon's predicament. Unable to stop himself, his body writhes. He has a desire to thrust, but retrains himself to avoid embarrassment.

Taking note of the second measurement, Mr. Tanaka grasps Gideon's cock much firmer in his hand and gently strokes.

Gideon looks down. "Uh, Mr. Tanaka?"

"I think we're way beyond formalities. Address me by my name, Satoro."

Turning his eyes back on the video, Gideon says, "What with the movie and all, well, if you keep doing that, it's embarrassing but you're going to make me come."

Satoro merely shrugs, replying nonchalantly, "Uh huh."

Gideon sees the closeup of the knife going into the woman's neck. He's unable to tear his eyes away from the video. *The kill scene.*

Satoro begins stroking faster.

"No," says Gideon. "It's not right."

Satoro halts. "What's not right?"

"Uh…" The knife goes in again. This time it's directed into the woman's chest. It mesmerizes Gideon. He stares for some time. Looking to the present conversation, Gideon can barely remember what he and Satoro were talking about. His thoughts sift through the drunken haze in his head.

"I can't do this…you're Kai's dad."

Satoro tilts his head, asking, "Would you feel better about it if I took your choice away?"

He squeezes Gideon firmer, sending chills through his body.

"Ah! What?" The entire room fills with tiny flecks of sparkling light. It floats all around him. Gideon's eyes flicker as he attempts to focus.

"You're tied up. I can make you come anytime I want."

Gideon's cock throbs in his hand.

"How does it feel, Gideon? Your body responding, wanting? All you need to do is surrender to it."

Satoro's voice is impatient. "Come on! I haven't got all night, do you want me to make the choice for you? Yes or no?"

Fuck!

Gideon flinches as Satoro barks, "Yes or no!"

"Uh..."

Satoro begins stroking softly. He can tell by Gideon's face, he's needy. It won't take much. "Do you want it harder?"

Gideon's eyes glimmer as they drop to meet Satoro's gaze. *He's not going to release me until he gets what he wants.*

Gideon finds himself slowly nodding.

"Say it!"

In little more than a whisper, Gideon replies, "Yes."

Gazing up at him, Satoro notices Gideon's eyes are dilated and flickering. He's stoned. Satoro gets up and positions himself behind him. He wraps one arm around

Gideon's hips to hold him steady. Unhooking the cock ring, he begins stroking more firmly. He pulls upward, twisting his wrist slightly as his grasp catches the edge of the head of Gideon's penis. With each upstroke, his fingertips pass over the glans.

Satoro's lips gently touch Gideon's ear. "Surrender." He continues to skillfully work Gideon.

"Oh God!" A tidal wave of intense pleasure rips through Gideon's core. It's fast and hard, overwhelming him. His body shivers violently, then suddenly goes limp.

Holding Gideon against him, Satoro pushes a button on the remote to lower the chain incrementally, allowing the blood to return to Gideon's arms.

After unhooking the shackles from the chain, Satoro says, "Lie down on the carpet."

Gideon drops to his knees. His arms feel like spaghetti.

Satoro helps him lie back.

In his hazy drunkenness, Gideon closes his eyes and passes out.

Satoro removes the shackles. He lifts Gideon's head to slip a small pillow underneath his neck. After drying the sweat from Gideon's body, he tosses the towel over the wet mess on the carpet. Covering Gideon with a large comforter, Satoro lays down next to him.

Gideon slips in and out of a dream state. The thick shag carpet gives him a sensation of floating.

He wakes briefly in the wee hours, feeling a shaking from Satoro's side of the blanket. Sensing, he's beating off, Gideon's too tired to care. He falls back asleep.

In the morning, Satoro wakes him and sends him back to Kai's room. As he heads back down to the second floor, Gideon can barely believe what happened. *Should I be embarrassed?* He has no idea how to feel about it. He decides it's best not to act weird about it. *Besides, no one will ever know.*

Standing at the mirror shaving, Satoro notices Houseki lurking in the doorway.

"Good morning, my pet."

"Good morning, Master."

"Is there something on your mind? I'm in a bit of a hurry. I'm meeting a vendor this morning."

"I just wanted to say goodbye before we go to Ms. Shelly's."

"You can always call me if anything comes up."

Houseki turns to leave, but hesitates.

She stands directly behind Satoro.

He looks up and asks impatiently, "What now?!"

She puts her fingertips on his upper abdomen and runs them down to his lower belly.

"I missed you last night."

He turns around to face her, then reaches up under her long black hair and grasps the back of her neck, pulling her toward him.

"No one will ever replace you, my pet."

Houseki smiles. Her master's infatuation with Gideon doesn't intimidate her. If anything, she and Oishii will have one more person to help share the brunt of Satoro's temper.

Houseki slowly drops to her knees as she takes Satoro in her mouth.

Satoro closes his eyes. *The vendor can wait.* "Harder," he says.

She tightens her grip around the base of his cock and strokes him firmly. Her mouth slides up and down his shaft, diving deep, allowing the head of his penis to slip past her throat. His thick girth cuts off her airway. As she pulls up, she holds her tongue rigid, rolling it over his sweet spot.

With his eyes closed, Satoro replays the memory of last night. Within minutes, Houseki is all but drowning in him.

She coughs, clearing her airway, then looks up at him.

Smiling down at her he says, "Evidently I missed you, too."

Punishment Fulfilled

With dazed looks on their faces, Gideon and Kai enter the grocery store. Besides a few guys at the beer coolers, the place seems to be filled with women and kids. Unlike Gideon, they all seem happy to be there. He grabs a grocery cart and turns to Kai. "What's first on the list?"

Kai doesn't hear a word. He's eyeballing the candy shelves opposite the check stands.

Tapping him on the shoulder, Gideon says, "Dude, the list."

"Right." Kai pulls the list from his pocket. "First thing is milk."

"Let's save the perishables for last. That way they won't warm up too much before we get them in the fridge."

"Good thinking. How do you know this stuff?"

"I just barely remember shopping with my mom. She always got vegetables first. When we got ice cream, it meant we were done."

"Did you ever grocery shop with your stepmother?"

"No way. You've seen her. She dresses like a skank."

They stop at the cereal aisle.

"Wow!" Kai says. "I didn't know there were so many different types of cereal." He grabs a box of chocolate puffs and hugs it.

"If your dad finds that, he might get pissed enough to send me home."

Kai's smile dissolves. He shoves the box back onto the shelf.

Gideon looks over at the smaller boxes across from the cereal.

"How about one of these? These boxes are small enough to stash somewhere in your room."

"Quick Starts?" Kai takes the box from Gideon. The picture of the icing-topped, fruit-filled pastries makes his mouth water.

"Have you had them?"

Gideon shakes his head. He picks up a box to look at the ingredients. Laughing, he says, "According to the ingredients, this is total kid crack."

Kai beams as he tosses the box in the cart. "Good enough for me."

Gideon pushes the cart down the aisle.

Twenty minutes later, they stand at the back of the store and check off all of the items on the list.

Gideon hears a familiar voice. He sees Mr. Smith shopping with his kids.

"Oh shit, duck!"

They hide behind the shopping cart as Mr. Smith walks past them. His three boys look to be about ten years old. The two skinny Asians are walking beside him. A pale boy with dirty brown hair lags behind, looking dejected.

Mr. Smith yells at him, "If I have to tell you again not to dawdle..." He whomps the boy hard across the back of his head.

The kid rubs his head but says nothing.

Kai whispers, "Did you see that?"

"Yeah," whispers, Gideon. "I can't believe any woman would have kids with him. Who would fuck that asshole?"

Kai frowns. "Gross, I don't even want to think about it."

When the Smiths turn the corner, Kai and Gideon make a run for the check stand.

Within a few days it's clear Kai is pretty useless in the kitchen. Having burned three meals, he's banned from cooking. Gideon is voluntold to do it.

Annoyed about it, Gideon pulls out a big knife and begins chopping onions. "Dude, I think this is one of those baby things where you fuck it all up so you don't have to do anything." He sets his knife down to flip the fish inside the oven.

Kai grins as he watches him cook. He finds it amusing, Gideon donning Oishii's apron, but he's not so stupid as to say anything about it.

Smirking, he says, "You're probably right."

Gideon glares at him. He's been fighting a migraine and could use some help.

"Make yourself useful and set the table."

Gideon drains the vegetables in a colander, then dumps them into a bowl with a pat of butter and a pinch of salt.

Kai watches him mix pickle relish, mayonnaise, garlic salt, and lemon juice into a bowl.

"Here, stir this up."

"What is it?"

"Tartar sauce. Just stir it and set the table, okay?"

"How'd you learn to make all this stuff?"

Gideon pulls the bread out of the broiler. "Ouch, dammit, that's hot!"

"You okay?"

He nods and grabs an oven mitt.

"I got the recipe in a cook book in the library at lunch."

While Kai sets the table, Gideon puts food on the plates, then hits the intercom. "Sir, dinner's ready."

Kai sighs heavily. "I'll be so glad when the girls are back."

"Why? Don't you like my cooking?"

"It's not that. It's just that all we do now is work. We don't have time for fun."

"I know. I miss them doing all this stuff, too."

"Absence makes one appreciate the other," says Satoro as he enters the room.

"Hi, Father."

"Kai, would you mind fetching a bottle of pinot noir, please?"

"I don't know how to find it. There are so many bottles in the cellar."

"Very well. Tonight, I want you to make a map charting out where all the different wines are by section. They're stored by type and vintage, so it's not a hard task."

"But, Father--"

"Stop acting like a baby! All you need to do is label the sections on your chart. A five year old could do it."

Kai decides he'd better do as he's told.

"Gideon, you will accompany me to deal with the obiats."

Gideon rubs his temples. "Sure."

"Migraine?"

"Uh huh."

Satoro gets up and leaves the room. He returns with two red pills and sets them down next to Gideon.

"Thanks." Gideon pops them into his mouth.

Satoro takes a bite of his dinner. "The fish is excellent."

"Kai picked it out."

"Excellent choice, son."

Kai smiles proudly.

After dinner, the boys clear the table. Gideon's head feels much better. He rinses the dishes and hands them to Kai to load in the dishwasher.

"Thanks for saying I helped with the fish."

"Thanks for not ratting me out for fibbing. I think he's tough on you when he's in a shitty mood."

"The fact that he isn't getting any may be affecting him."

Gideon laughs. "Oh man, I didn't think of that."

A half hour later, Satoro and Gideon leave Kai with the task of charting the wine cellar. They head out to tend to the obiats.

Gideon follows Satoro to the iron gates directly across from his office. Behind each gate is a dark tunnel. It's creepy.

Satoro enters his code on the left gate.

"Where does the other tunnel go?"

"Always so inquisitive, aren't you?

Gideon decides not to press him. He's already been yelled at earlier today.

As they enter the tunnel, the lights come on automatically. Along one wall is a painting of a huge reptile. The body is red and black with gold scales. The tail goes on for a while before they come upon the leg of the animal.

"Is it…a dragon?"

"It is."

"Why dragons?"

"I have a fondness for them. They're fearless. Not to mention they sit at the top of the food chain."

Every twenty feet, Gideon notices there's an arched buttress supporting the tunnel. On the backside of each one is a ceiling vent. He decides he'll take a walk out onto the property in the daylight to see if he can track the other tunnel to see where it leads.

When they reach the head of the dragon, Gideon moves this way and that, watching the eyes follow him. The dragon's orange and blue flames appear to leap off the wall.

"It's cool."

"It is, isn't it? Come..." Satoro leads him to a door with a key pad. A hand written note is taped to it.

"Who's it from?"

"Houseki. She came by today to pick up some spices. You and Kai were probably out shopping. It says she bathed and fed the obiats, but didn't feed Zen."

"Doesn't she like Zen?"

Satoro chuckles. "Zen spits at her out of jealousy."

Gideon laughs. "That's messed up."

Satoro enters his code and motions for Gideon to enter.

The room is near dark. Only a few candles provide any light. As Gideon looks around, he notices the same windows that he and Kai had seen when they were on their quest to find the camo building.

"Are we inside the camo building?"

"You know about this place?"

Gideon nods. "We went for a walk in the back yard and stumbled onto it months ago." He lies. "We thought it was the gardener's storage or something."

"Let me show you one of my prize pets, shall I?"

Gideon follows Satoro into a room filled with lush green plants. In the center is a woman sleeping on her back. She's one of the most fascinating creatures he's ever seen. Her entire body is tattooed with scales, the same scales that are painted on the wall in the tunnel.

"She's a dragon?" whispers Gideon.

Satoro nods.

Gideon steps closer to inspect the gold flecks of paint tattooed between the scales. As she breathes, the scales move slightly. He notices her limbs are locked into place. Each is held by a golden hand with fingers which wrap around her wrists and ankles. He squats down to look underneath her. The hands suspending her, are forged on a platform. They hold Zen's body like some kind of sacrificial creature.

When Gideon stands, he sees Zen's eyes are open. Her green and gold irises stare back at him. She has reptilian eyes.

She smiles at him. Her eyes dart around to look for her master.

"She's amazing. How did you get her eyes like that?"

"It's a tattoo process, very tricky, not to mention painful. She likes you; I can tell. Put your finger in her mouth."

"Seriously, tattooed eyeballs?"

"I have an associate who specializes in it. Go ahead, put your finger in her mouth."

Gideon feels apprehensive about it. "What if she bites me?"

"She can't bite you."

"What do you mean she can't bite me?"

"Just do it!"

Reluctantly, Gideon sticks his finger in the woman's mouth. She latches onto it, sucking. The sensation is strange. Her mouth is pillowy and soft. She's without any teeth. Her cheeks begin vibrating and her tongue rolls across his finger. It is as if she is gently milking it with her mouth. The vibration gets increasingly intense.

"How is she doing that?"

Satoro grins salaciously. "She's been surgically altered. And not just her mouth."

Noticing she has yet to address Satoro, Gideon asks, "Doesn't she speak?"

"No, her vocal cords are cut. She's a sex instrument, Gideon. An incredible one at that, but nothing more."

It's sinking in how incredibly rich and powerful Satoro is. *He literally had a human being changed into a sex toy.* Gideon wonders what Satoro would do to him if he ever crosses him.

"Would you like to see the tape of her body and eyes being tattooed?"

"You have a tape of it?!"

Playfully Satoro says, "Of course, it won't come without an indebtness."

"Any chance you'd extend me a freebie?"

"Not when it comes to you. You'll owe me a carnal favor once I decide what it is."

As much as he doesn't want to owe Satoro anything, he can't resist.

"Yeah, okay."

"Good. First, we'll wash and feed Zen."

Pulling his finger from her mouth, Gideon asks, "How does she eat without teeth?"

"We drop a tube down her throat and pour it in."

Gnarly...

Satoro heads down a concrete stairway to fetch a wash bowl and towels.

When he returns, he shows Gideon how to bath his prized obiat.

Satoro asks Gideon to wait with Zen while he looks in on his two other obiats.

While waiting, Gideon glances around the room and up at the reinforced ceiling. Knowing now that the structure of the building is far bigger than just the storage shed from outside, he ponders how far underground it extends.

Satoro stands between his other prized pets. Both girls are sleeping soundly. He kisses each one on the forehead, then turns away, closing the door behind him.

"Perhaps you would like your own obiat, someday."

Gideon glances in Satoro's direction. "As beautiful and amazing as Zen is, I don't know if I'm ready for that kind of responsibility."

"It's a commitment, certainly. Like owning a dog or anything else worth having."

"It seems like a lot more work than just a dog. Dogs wash their own butts."

Satoro chuckles. "Indeed they do."

Gideon gently strokes Zen's cheek. "But say I actually wanted an obiat, how would I get one?"

"It depends on who you know. You know me, and that can be useful for just about anything."

Twenty-six hours later, Gideon finds himself in Satoro's secret room, naked and shackled. Satoro is 'cashing in' on the carnal favor he agreed to.

"Would you like to beat the obiats tomorrow?"

Gideon ponders whether to put himself in even more debt.

"What will it cost me?"

"I think what you're really asking is whether or not it will hurt."

Gideon nods. It's as if Satoro knows what he's thinking before he does.

Satoro holds brandy to his lips.

Gideon takes a sip, savoring it before swallowing. He already feels the effects, yet he's just barely tasted it.

Satoro turns his back, then moves across the room.

Gideon watches him as he begins digging through cabinet drawers.

"So, will it? Hurt, I mean?"

As Satoro turns around, Gideon sees he has a leather strap in his hand. The inch-wide rawhide is about as long as Satoro's forearm. He slowly drags it across the side of Gideon's face.

"It depends on how hard I wield it. Your body will tell me how hard you want it."

Want it?

"What if my body doesn't want it?"

Satoro's eyes wander down Gideon's abdomen. His hips are forward and he's hard. *He wants it.*

Satoro moves behind him, reaches down across the front of his abdomen and takes hold of Gideon's cock. He pets it with the soft rawhide strap.

With his lips against Gideon's ear, he asks, "Aren't you just a teensy-weensy bit curious to know what it feels like?"

Knowing Satoro will have his way regardless, Gideon slowly nods.

Satoro begins stroking him firmer and faster, then lightly smacks him across his belly with the strap.

Gideon lets out an involuntary squeal.

Satoro uncuffs one of Gideon's hands.

"Let me see you masturbate."

Embarrassed, Gideon hesitates.

Satoro whips the strap hard across his buttocks.

"Ow, fuck!"

"Do it now, or the strikes will get harder. You might not like where it's going next."

Reluctantly, Gideon begins stroking himself.

Satoro continues hitting him, moving incrementally down his abdomen.

"I'd advise you to make yourself come before I reach your penis. If you do, I'll stop. Otherwise, I won't, and I'm afraid it will sting like a bitch."

The slaps get progressively harder and move slowly down Gideon's body.

Frantic to come, Gideon jerks faster but has trouble concentrating through the pain.

"Focus!" Satoro growls.

Gideon closes his eyes. He tightens his grip and concentrates on pleasuring himself. The blows to his body seem to intensify everything going on inside him. A minute later, he feels a familiar surge rising inside.

"Oh shhh!" His body tenses as he milks himself through the waves of an intense orgasm, spurting all over the carpet.

When it's over, Satoro unbuckles him.

"Well done."

Exhausted, Gideon asks, "What was the point to that?"

"To prepare you to beat the obiats, of course. You have to experience first hand what it's like."

Confused, Gideon asks, "What do you mean?"

"Depending on how you use a strap, you instill pleasure, fear, or pain."

The next night, Kai's stuck on the phone with Chantelle for several hours.

Satoro decides with Kai tied up on the phone, he'll take Gideon to the camo building.

As Gideon uses the strap on Zen, he asks, "Why does she look so content?"

"She's happy with any physical contact. She lives in a dark, lonely world. Any attention, be it good or bad, is perceived by her to be good."

Gideon frowns. *It kind of takes all the fun out of it.*

The following morning over breakfast, Gideon mentions to Kai that it seems as though he's always stuck on the phone with Chantelle.

"I really don't mind."

"What does she talk about for so long?"

Kai shrugs. "Her friends at school, her cheer routines, lots of random stuff."

"That would lull me right to sleep."

Kai blurts out defensively, "Which is why you don't have a girlfriend!"

"Yeah, well, have you even got past first base?"

Eavesdropping, Satoro makes a mental note to ask Gideon not to encourage Kai to get physically involved with Chantelle.

Later that evening, while Kai is busy on the phone, Satoro tells Gideon he wants to talk to him in his office.

The two men chat about Chantelle.

"She isn't attractive or smart."

"She is, if you're into twinkies." Gideon laughs.

"I'm serious." Satoro laments. "Chantelle has no chance of getting into a prestigious college. She doesn't fit the profile of anyone I would want Kai seriously involved with. It would be a disaster if she became pregnant by him."

"Oh..." The idea disturbs Gideon. If she got pregnant, they'd never get rid of her. "I haven't thought about her getting pregnant. If she did, what would you do about it?"

Satoro gives him a somber look. "I think you already know the answer to that."

He'd kill her.

Satoro sighs. "If the time comes when she needs taking care of, can I rely on your confidentiality?"

Raising his eyebrow, Gideon asks, "Are you suggesting I do it?"

"Absolutely not. Just support the notion that it was a random act of a lunatic. Neither one of us would be involved."

BIRTHDAY PRESENT

After practically living with the Tanaka's for a year, Gideon sits in his room trying to come up with an idea for Satoro's birthday. Staring at a blank sheet for half an hour, it strikes him, the perfect gift, but he'll need to visit Shelly's drug supplier.

The evening before the big day, Gideon feels anxious. He's put off bringing up the subject due to Satoro having been in a foul mood. Tonight is his last opportunity.

Having finished dinner, Gideon and Satoro listen while Kai rambles on about Chantelle's amazing cheerleading skills. Despite making an effort to be more involved in Kai's life, Satoro seems miserably uninterested in Chantelle.

"She's been cheering for almost two years," says Kai. "It's not fair that she's always stuck in the back row."

Gideon glances at him. *She sucks, dude.* He turns to Satoro. "Sir, would you be up for a short expedition tomorrow morning around seven? I have a birthday gift for you."

Satoro glances at Kai. "Did you tell him about it?"

"I don't see what the big deal is, father. He asked about it months ago." Kai shrugs, adding, "Besides, everyone has a birthday."

Satoro turns his attention on Gideon. "Thank you, but I already have everything I need."

Gideon gently pushes, "If I may say so, it's not about the stuff. Don't you want to know how much you're appreciated?"

Satoro's eyes twinkle. Gideon knows exactly how to draw him in. "Very well, if it means that much to you, I'll bite."

"Really?! I mean great...you'll want to wear long sleeves, and tennis shoes."

"Tennis shoes?"

Satoro yells over at the kitchen door, "Oishii! Do I own tennis shoes?"

"Yes, sir."

"Thanks, Oishii!" yells Gideon. "May I be excused? I have some 'wrapping' to do."

The next morning Satoro wanders into the kitchen a few minutes before seven.

Koko trails behind him and sits in front of his empty bowl. Satoro picks it up and fills it with dog food.

The dog sniffs it, then looks at him, expecting something better.

Satoro's eyes narrow. He grumbles, "They eat dogs in some countries."

Koko hurries out of the kitchen with his tail down. He'll find a more charitable human.

There's a fresh pot of coffee on the stove. Satoro helps himself to a cupful. As he takes the first sip, Gideon rushes in. Carrying his backpack, he appears slightly disheveled.

"You're right on time," Satoro says.

Gideon glances at the clock. "Are you ready?"

Satoro nods.

As they head outside, Satoro tosses his keys to Gideon. "You drive."

They head east for twenty minutes, then turn onto a dirt road that takes them deep into the woods. Several miles in, they come to a dead end.

Satoro gets out of the car and sees the pathway heading into the forest. "Are we going for a hike?"

"Yep."

Retrieving his backpack from the trunk, Gideon digs inside and pulls out a green can. "May I spray you?"

"Excuse me?"

Gideon holds up a can of Deet.

Frowning, Satoro asks, "Is that...bug spray?"

"That's right. See?" Gideon closes his eyes and lightly sprays his own face and neck.

He offers the can to Satoro.

"Certainly not! It smells awful!"

"The smell is temporary. It'll keep the mosquitos off of you."

Satoro slaps the back of his neck, "Shit!"

Gideon tries, but fails to hold back a grin.

Grabbing the can, Satoro sprays himself, grumbling, "Don't think I'll forget this."

Gideon tosses his backpack over his shoulder. "Let's go."

The woods are cool and shaded. Sunlight peeks through the trees, casting sporadic beams of light onto the pathway. The air smells heavenly. The soil under their feet is soft, thick with moss.

About a quarter of a mile in, the path narrows. Gideon takes the lead.

Twenty yards beyond that, he stops and turns to face Satoro. Satoro looks past him. Vines are blocking the path ahead.

Feeling uneasy, Gideon stammers, "I hope you don't think this gift is stupid."

Satoro puts his hand on Gideon's shoulder. "Success shouldn't always be measured on an outcome. Knowing you did your best is all anyone can expect."

Gideon pulls down the vines, revealing the hidden meadow. "Happy birthday, Satoro."

A vast carpet of wildflowers extends across the enormous field. That alone would have been enough to take one's breath away, but when he sees her naked body against the giant lone redwood tree, Satoro gasps in awe.

Reading the look on Satoro's face, Gideon knows he's done well. He glances over at her, too. She looks lovely, tied spread eagled to the giant tree.

Satoro takes it all in. *What a talent Gideon has! He must have worked all night putting this together.*

Gideon steps forward, but Satoro pulls his shoulder back. "Wait, I want to look at it a moment longer, before anything changes."

"No rush." Gideon steps back and sets down his backpack.

Satoro drinks in the view for several minutes, then turns and says, "Where did you find her?"

Gideon hesitates. If Satoro knew Olivia sells crack, he might think that she's a user, not just a dealer. He lies. "She supplies Shelly with diet pills. She's some kind of pharmacy rep."

Gideon unpacks a small video camera and hands it to Satoro.

"Just push the red button when you want to record and push it again to stop. If the green light is on, you're still in record mode."

Satoro nods. He heads for the meadow, videotaping as he walks.

Following him, Gideon hears the bees hard at work collecting pollen. It sounds as though each has a kazoo, and all are playing the same tune.

When they reach the base of the tree, the girl's blue eyes are fixated on them. She's drooling slightly from the gag in her mouth.

Olivia's creamy white complexion and long, cherry colored hair make her a perfect candidate for the tree. She's a Venus for sure. Her eyes seem to be begging them to set her free. Thankfully, she isn't spoiling it by pleading or whining. Gideon warned her what would happen if she wasn't docile.

He gave her a ruffie of LSD and ketamine. Two drugs she sells on the street. Gideon thought it only fitting that she experience the effects first hand.

Satoro asks, "What's her name?"

"Olivia."

Touching her cheek, Satoro says softly, "Ooh-livia." He slides his hands over her velvety hips and down the side of her thighs. He cups her small breasts.

"Natural breasts, I like that."

Satoro's hands slide between her legs. "You're very beautiful. I want to fuck you."

Olivia closes her eyes tightly and shakes her head "no."

Satoro turns to Gideon. "She's not wet enough. Get on your knees and make her wet."

Gideon kneels down. He's thankful the bugs haven't invaded her. He begins licking, then quickly backs off, making an unpleasant face and wiping his mouth on his shirt.

Satoro frowns. "What? What is it? Does she taste bad?"

"Not exactly. I sprayed her with Deet this morning. I emptied an entire can on her body."

Satoro bursts out laughing. "Keep licking!"

A minute later Gideon wipes his lips on his shirt, then backs up.

Satoro unbuckles his belt, then pulls his cock free.

"Get the video camera." He begins stroking himself as he waits for Gideon.

Gideon retrieves a condom out of a small side pocket in his backpack and offers it to Satoro.

Satoro scowls at him.

"You'll want to wear it," Gideon insists. "She's clean, but just the same, I can't exactly see way up inside her."

Grumbling, Satoro snatches the condom out of Gideon's hand. "You can't exactly see a disease, now can you?"

"Well," says Gideon smugly, "I sprayed Lysol up there and then douched her out with one of those box kits." He picks up the camera. "C'mon, we're rolling."

Satoro turns to him. His voice is sharp. "Keep my face out of this, understood?"

"Yeah, only your body parts will be famous."

Satoro faces Olivia. He asks her softly, "Are you a good girl, Olivia?"

She looks up at him crying and shivering, but doesn't respond.

"Do you want to do it with me, Olivia?"

She turns her head away.

"Answer me," he says calmly.

Nothing.

He smacks her hard across the face.

Olivia screams under the gag.

"Was that a yes?"

Afraid he'll hit her again, she nods.

Slowly, Satoro slides his cock inside her.

Olivia attempts to buck him off.

Satoro clutches her face in one hand. "Hold still."

Gideon zooms in to get a closer view.

Taunting her, Satoro asks, "Do you like it hard?"

Olivia shakes her head "no."

Satoro slaps her again.

Annoyed, Gideon says impatiently, "Yes, Olivia. It's always yes, for fuck sake! How lame can you be?!"

Satoro begins ramming her hard. In a matter of minutes, he unleashes an orgasm, then quickly pulls out, careful to hang onto the condom.

Gideon shuts off the camera. When he turns around, Satoro's gone.

He picks up the backpack, then walks around to the other side of the tree. He finds Satoro sitting on a huge boulder.

"Here, take this." Satoro hands him the condom, which he tied off.

"Gee, thanks." It feels grossly warm.

"We can't leave anything behind."

Gideon nods, then sets the backpack down beside the rock. He places the condom in one of the side pockets. Reaching inside the main compartment, he pulls out two plastic champagne glasses. He hands them to Satoro.

"That's an excellent bottle of champagne you have there."

"It's not from your collection. Oishi told me what you like, that I could actually afford."

"I'm impressed. Where did you get the money?"

"Shelly paid for it."

"Shelly?"

"Uh huh. She was passed out, so I took cash out of the food money box to buy it. There's a ton of money in it. It's not like she ever buys food."

"Why won't she buy food?"

"Food has to be earned. I hated what I had to do to get it."

The comment alarms Satoro. "When you say 'earned,' what did you do?"

"She'd make me clean up puke...scrub piss off her bathroom walls. None of her dates could hit the toilet bowl. Anyway, I stopped being her mutt at twelve."

"What did you do for food?"

Hanging his head in shame, Gideon says, "I dug in the trash cans after lunch at school."

Satoro realizes Gideon has been through far more than he could have imagined. He's amazed that he turned out as smart and interesting as he is.

"You shouldn't have had to put up with that."

Gideon shrugs. "I survived." Seeing the concerned look on Satoro's face, he changes the subject. "Anyway, just before my dad died, someone bought all of his patents, so the money in that box, it's rightfully mine."

Gideon fiddles with getting the wrapper off the champagne bottle.

"Why doesn't Shelly just put the food money in the bank?"

"I suppose because then the attorney would know she isn't using the money to buy food. That would be proof she isn't taking care of me properly, violating her contract."

"Do you know how much your dad sold his patents for?"

Shrugging, Gideon says, "I don't know. Dad was pleased about the sale, so maybe as much as million."

Satoro smiles. *Eleven million to be exact.*

"Tell me again? What would violating the contract do?"

"It would prevent her from getting money for our living expenses. Mr. Spencer, my dad's attorney, would probably turn the money over to me. Then I could pay you back for all the money you've spent to help me with my classes and materials."

"I'll arrange it."

Gideon raises an eyebrow. "What are you saying?"

"We'll frame her. We'll open a bank account with funds under Shelly's name, then anonymously notify Mr. Spencer. If Shelly's accused of fraud, Mr. Spencer will be obligated to fire her. It's as simple as that."

"Yeah, but how are you going to prove it?"

"You let me worry about that. Are you going to open that bottle or are we just going to die of thirst here?"

Untwisting the wire, Gideon pulls up on the cork. There's a 'pop,' followed by the sound of fizz as gold liquid bubbles spill over the rim of the bottle.

Gideon fills the glasses.

"Happy birthday, Satoro."

They each take a sip.

"I have something else for you."

Gideon pulls out a black leather box wrapped with a white, slightly smashed bow, and hands it to Satoro.

"What's this?"

"It's your present. Open it."

Satoro sets his glass on the rock and takes the box.

"Remind me to flog you later, will you?" He hands Gideon the bow. He already knows what's inside by the insignia on the outside of the box.

He opens it and smiles. "How did you know?"

"I borrowed the picture hanging on your office wall…"

Satoro pulls the knife out of the box, mumbling, "Borrowed?...I'm definitely punishing you." Admiring the dagger, Satoro adds, "This is quite amazing."

Gideon leans closer to look at it as well.

"They did an excellent job on this replica," Satoro says. "Very impressive indeed. I'll tell you the story about that picture some time. Unfortunately, the dagger was destroyed."

"Well, I just thought…you'd need something to kill her with." Gideon tilts his head in Olivia's direction.

Satoro raises an eyebrow. This is the second time today Gideon has truly surprised him.

"You want me to kill Olivia?"

"Yes, well, unless you want to make a pet out of her."

"She's very beautiful, but it's not that simple. Developing a pet takes years. There's a brainwashing of sorts. It's complicated."

"Have you ever thought about speeding up the process?"

"How so?"

"By removing the part of the brain that doesn't want to be a pet."

"That's an interesting thought. A discussion to have for another time, but I'm interested in having it."

"Well, if you want to kill Olivia, I'd be happy to videotape it for your memoirs. I'll even dispose of her body."

Turning the dagger over, Satoro reads the inscription. "Satoro, Happy Birthday. Love, Gideon."

He feels a twinge in his chest. All he ever wanted is unfolding before him, but keeping it comes with more challenges. *This could very well change Gideon.* Thinking about it, Satoro decides he'll mentor Gideon, so he doesn't make stupid mistakes.

"All right, then. Let's finish our champagne first, shall we?"

Satoro intentionally sips his champagne slowly. He's enjoying the day and is in no hurry.

"Let me ask you, Gideon. What is it about killing that you think you like?"

"Um, revenge, I think. Just pure revenge."

"Is that so? Well, if that's the case, why then would you want to kill Olivia? She hasn't done anything for you to seek vengeance."

Not wanting to disclose his reasons for killing Olivia, Gideon replies, "What are you getting at?"

"I'm trying to make a point. My hunch is you're a born killer who likes to kill for the simple enjoyment of doing it. My question is, do you know why?"

"But I haven't hurt anyone," he lies. If Satoro knew all the terrible things he'd done, he may not want him around.

"Not yet, but you will. And many, I can tell."

Gideon wonders if he's right. *Can he really see all of that in me?*

"You know you will. There's no reason to get perturbed about it. Embrace what you are and find a good purpose for it. We are who we are, not always by our own doing."

Thoughtfully, Gideon asks, "All right then, what's a good purpose for killing people?"

Satoro watches him take a large gulp of his champagne. He makes a mental note to teach him the art of consuming it, so he can develop him into a true connoisseur.

"People, is it? It seems to me you have a particular preference." Satoro takes a couple of small sips to match Gideon's big one.

"Uh, okay...women."

"Now we're getting somewhere."

"Why are we talking about this? We should be killing Olivia."

"We? You mean me, don't you? What's the rush? She's not going anywhere."

Gideon shrugs impatiently.

"The reason we're talking about this is because you should know who's going to satisfy that hunger when it comes up. You don't want to take control of someone only to find she isn't what you want. Then you'd go out and find another and have not one, but two victims on your hands. Two bodies to get rid of. That's very risky."

"I never thought about it that way."

"You've thought about killing others besides Shelly, haven't you?"

"Yes."

"What is it about them that makes you want to kill them?"

Satoro senses Gideon's never thought about this before.

"Take a minute to think about it. I've got all day."

After much thought, Gideon decides it's about taking his power back. Ms. Pinkberry used her body to try to manipulate him. *All I did was relieve her of it.*

"I don't like how women use their sex appeal to control a man."

"Do you think all women are bad?"

Gideon shakes his head. "No. Like, Houseki and Oishii, they're good. I'd never want to hurt them."

"I'm curious, what is it about blood that fascinates you?"

"How do you know about that?"

"Just answer the question. What about it fascinates you?"

"The color mostly. It's the shade of life."

"What do you mean?"

"There's nothing quite like it. The cells change color over time depending on how alive they are."

"Do you cut yourself, Gideon?"

"What? No!"

"You've got quite a collection of blood. Where'd you get it?"

Impatient, Gideon frowns. "I never told anyone, so how did you find out about it?"

"When I first saw you on the video tapes, I asked an associate to do a background check on you. He said due to your age, he wouldn't find much. So, he went to your house. He found your hiding spot in the back of your closet."

Hearing this, Gideon's eyes widen. "You have a spy?"

Satoro chuckles, "You don't seriously think I'd allow you to hang out with my son without knowing everything about you?"

"Why wait so long to tell me about it?"

Satoro shrugs. "I don't know. I felt a little guilty about it. It was an infringement of your privacy."

Gideon tries to imagine it. Some stranger sneaking around his home.

"Was Shelly home?"

Satoro nods. "Sleeping."

Passed out is more like it.

"You still haven't said where all that blood came from."

Gideon fidgets uncomfortably. "Okay, when Shelly passes out, I sometimes bleed her."

"You what?"

"She passes out for days. I could literally drain all the blood out of her body if I wanted to."

"I see. When is the last time you did this?"

Gideon looks down at his feet.

Satoro nudges him, "Come on, tell me."

Sheepishly, Gideon replies, "Two nights ago."

Satoro laughs. "So, you bleed her on a regular basis, like a goat or something?"

Gideon hangs his head. "Uh huh."

"That's a bit twisted, isn't it?"

"I guess."

Stretching his arms, Satoro asks, "So, is that it? That's what infatuates you? Just the color?"

"I don't know. I haven't really thought about it."

"Okay, we'll work on figuring that one out together. Let's kill Olivia, shall we?"

Satoro finishes his champagne, then stands.

Gideon grabs the camera and his backpack. The thought of Satoro killing Olivia sends butterflies through him.

"Satoro?"

"Yes?"

"What do you like about killing?"

Handing Gideon his empty glass he replies, "Hm. I can make someone experience death either joyously or painfully. If I want them to be horrified, I can terrify them. If I want them to be calm, I'll send them to the afterlife peacefully, even willfully sometimes."

"You mean you like the control?"

Satoro grins. "This is what I've come to admire about you. You insightfully see beneath the surface of one's psyche. But what you call control, I like to think of as guidance."

"Uh huh," says Gideon sarcastically. He stashes the glasses and the champagne wrapper back in his backpack, then follows Satoro.

Standing in front of Olivia, Satoro admires his new dagger. He asks, "How do you want this to go?"

Gideon shrugs. "It's your birthday. You decide."

Satoro looks down at the obvious bulge below Gideon's belly.

"This is stimulating you, isn't it?"

Gideon turns a shade of pink. "Yeah."

"We have that in common. Let's decide her end together." Satoro places his hand on Gideon's shoulder, then says softly, "Before we begin, you need to know there's no going back. Once you take a life, you own it. She will be on our shoulders, yours and mine, forever."

Gideon feels his stomach flip. It's the first time Satoro actually verbalized any kind of irreversible connection with him.

"I understand."

He walks a few paces back. He sets the camera on top of his backpack, facing Olivia. The two men keep their backs to the camera.

Standing side-by-side, they admire her.

Olivia whimpers.

Gideon looks to Satoro. "Can we bleed her?"

"Certainly. Let's start by slicing the radial artery."

Gideon watches as Satoro feels the inside of Olivia's wrist for her radial artery. Once he locates it, he has Gideon feel it as well. Her pulse is beating fast. Satoro punctures the artery twice in a crisscross cut.

Olivia lets out a muffled scream. Satoro slaps her and tells her to remain quiet. She falls into a quiet whimper.

Gideon's eyes grow wide with excitement. He watches as blood spurts out of Olivia's wrist in unison with her heart beat.

Satoro hands him the dagger and tilts his head, signaling him to do the other side.

When Gideon's certain he has the correct location, he makes the first cut.

Olivia lets out another muffled scream. Gideon quickly makes the second cut, crossing over the first. He glances at Satoro, who's smiling at him with approval.

"You're a natural, Gideon."

Thrusting his hand under the flow of blood, Gideon catches it, then rubs it across Olivia's chest.

"She's lovely, isn't she?"

"Yes, Gideon, she's wonderful."

He hands the knife back to Satoro.

It occurs to Satoro, sharing this kill with Gideon is an enormous turn on.

"These are the smaller arteries that will bleed out the victim but still keep them alive a bit longer. They're called the anterior and posterior tibial arteries."

Satoro pierces Olivia on each side of her lower leg, making a small crisscross cut on each side. With each piercing, Olivia screams, but both men seem oblivious to her. Blood spurts from her leg. Satoro hands the dagger to Gideon.

Gideon quickly pierces her other posterior tibial artery. He has trouble finding the anterior tibial artery, then moves farther down Olivia's lower leg where he easily finds it. He barely hears her high-pitched squeal behind the sound of Satoro's, "Well done!"

He hands the dagger back to him.

"If you're in more of a hurry, you can always go for the larger arteries, such as the femoral artery right here." Satoro feels in the crux of Olivia's hip down to the center of her leg and stabs her.

Blood flows out rapidly, spurting like an open faucet. He holds the dagger out to Gideon.

Unable to stop himself, Gideon thrust his hands under the flow of blood, staring transfixedly at the life pouring out of Olivia's body.

Watching him, Satoro says, "She's got little time, Gideon. I need you to pay attention."

Gideon grabs the dagger and quickly stabs Olivia in the other leg. Blood spurts, but nowhere near as rapidly as the first side. He glances at Olivia, who appears to be in a dream state. He hands the dagger back to Satoro.

"Lastly, there's the carotid artery. Use this technique when you're in a hurry and there's no time. It gets the job done quickly."

Satoro pulls Olivia's unconscious head to the side and stabs her deep in her neck. Blood dribbles out of her neck slowly. He hands Gideon the dagger.

Suspecting that Olivia is most likely dead now, Gideon stabs her in the neck anyway. Nothing comes out. Her faucet is dry.

Gideon backs up and shuts off the camera.

Satoro glances at him. "Do you want help with her body?"

Gideon stuffs the camera in his backpack. "No, it's okay. I'll drop you off at the house, then I'll come back and take care of it."

Concerned, Satoro asks, "How do you plan to deal with it?"

"We have a huge incinerator in the basement." Gideon turns to him and insists, "Let me do this."

Satoro considers whether or not he should let Gideon do it by himself.

"Do you like fucking dead women?"

"What?!" Gideon frowns disgustedly. "No!"

Satoro chuckles at himself for teasing him. His voice becomes stern. "All right. I'll allow it, but if you run into trouble..."

"-yeah, I know. I'll call you immediately."

Satoro hands Gideon the dagger. "Make sure you come right back to the house when it's all cleaned up. Oishii has a small birthday dinner planned and if I have to endure it, you and Kai can suffer right along with me."

Gideon shoves the bloody dagger inside his backpack next to the crumbled white bow, before zipping it up. *Steak and cake...sure, I'll suffer.*

Satoro heads toward the path. Gideon follows him. As they make their way to the car, Satoro turns toward him. "I insist you attend my after party as well."

Gideon looks up inquisitively. Satoro raises and lowers his eyebrows, then continues down the path. Gideon rolls his eyes. *Right...*

Eight hours later, Gideon finds himself at the after party in the 'Puf' room. He nicknamed it 'Puf' on account of the dragons on the wall. Setting his backpack on the credenza, he begins unpacking it.

Satoro opens a bottle of champagne. "I could buy myself anything for my birthday, except the one thing I particularly want."

"Oh, yeah? And what's that?"

Satoro offers Gideon a glass of champagne, then pulls a pair of handcuffs from his pocket. "Wear these willfully, but most of all, unconditionally."

Gideon accepts the glass of champagne, then sniffs it suspiciously.

Satoro chuckles. "I assure you, it's only champagne."

"Uh huh, how many times have I heard that?"

Staring at the handcuffs dangling from Satoro's hand, Gideon's eyes shift to the red leather box in the middle of the table.

"What's in the box?"

"If you put these on, you'll find out."

"Is it actually up to me? You're giving me a choice?"

"No, I'm giving you the opportunity to feel as though you do."

Gideon seats himself in a red velvet chair. "Will it hurt?"

"Only in so much as you fight it. I'd be more inclined to go easier if you come along willingly."

Gideon's thoughts return to what Houseki and Oishii said to him at that first dinner. 'Mr. Tanaka needs to feel he's in control of the situation.' It occurs to him this isn't real control. Not in the way Satoro wants it. If it was, there'd be no need to ask for it. He lets out a deep sigh. *This is what my life has become...Satoro's personal plaything.*

Glancing at the backpack in the corner, he sees the bloody bow sitting next to it. *But if I get to kill...*

He sets his champagne down and offers up his wrists.

Follow the saga. Take a sneak peek into Salacious's next provocative book in the Gideon Rising series.

GIDEON RISING book 2, OBLIGATION

"I don't like being pressured."

"I've never made you do anything. Think about it objectively, Gideon. I've taken advantage, yes, but usually not without compromise on my part."

"What does that mean?"

"It means had I wanted to, I could have taken you a hundred times by now. I'm more interested in your pleasure than mine. But regardless, we made an agreement and you agreed to it. You've always had a choice."

He's right. He could do what Satoro asks, or walk away from it all. Its always been his choice to stay.

"I want more time with Kai."

Satoro asks jokingly, "Shall we kill Chantelle, then?"

Gideon instinctively grins, then catches himself. "Uh, no. He'd assume it was me."

Satoro's voice softens. "I want to take you away with me. Me, you and Kai."

A trip? He's never been anywhere in his life.

"Away where?"

"Any place you want to go."

Gideon can't decide who has won here. *Is he really that desperate to keep me?*

"Please, Gideon, come to dinner tonight. We'll make plans."

"No, I…I already have plans," he lies. He doesn't want to give in so easily.

There's a long pause. *Satoro's not used to being told 'no.'*

"Tomorrow, then."

"K, bye." Gideon abruptly hangs up.

www.ingramcontent.com/pod-product-compliance
Lightning Source LLC
Chambersburg PA
CBHW070830120626
46556CB00002B/707

* 9 7 8 1 7 3 6 6 6 4 4 1 4 *